T0368749

A CLASS REUNION

Clarence Willis

authorHOUSE®

AuthorHouse™
1663 Liberty Drive
Bloomington, IN 47403
www.authorhouse.com
Phone: 1-800-839-8640

First published by AuthorHouse 7/27/2011

ISBN: 978-1-4634-3381-9 (sc)
ISBN: 978-1-4634-3382-6 (e)

This book dedicated to my daughter
NancyLeigh who thinks her dad
can do anything — even write a book

ONE

THE MEMBERS OF the Seaford, Delaware high school class of 1984 were attending their first reunion on June 22nd 1989. They had decided when graduating, that they would have a reunion every five years as long as there were five or more members of the graduating class who agreed to attend each reunion. They had a total of $835.00 in their five year reunion bank account.

Their first reunion had a total of 45 of the 56 class members attending. Eleven members of the class were not in attendance. Fred Dyson was in the US Air Force and stationed at the Randolph Field AFB. He was unable to attend as he was on duty at the base located in Universal City, Texas. He did respond to the committee after having received the invitation and wished them all a fun evening and told them he was sorry that he could not attend.

There were five members, who failed to respond to the

invitation and did not attend the reunion, John Bennett, Franklin Morris, Douglas Weaver, and Betty (Smith) Bennett.

The only classmates that failed to attend the reunion after confirming that they would be there were Harriet O'Brien, Harry Black, and Robert Miller.

Robert Miller owned a computer Internet development company. He reported that he was still unmarried and lived in Wilmington, Delaware. He was reported as having been seen in Seaford a few days prior to the reunion, but he failed to attend the reunion and he also failed to advise anyone that he would not be attending the reunion as he had originally planned.

Harry Black lived in Tampa, Florida and was a musician. He had returned his invitation and stated that he would be in Ocean City, Maryland with a band and would make sure that he came over to the reunion. He failed to attend and there was no further word from him.

Harriet O'Brien was a very popular girl of the class and a high school cheerleader. She was very active in all high school athletic programs. She was a star basketball player and the team captain. Two days before the reunion, Harriet was found dead by strangulation, in a wooded area east of Seaford in an area locally called, The Island. The Island was a favorite lover's lane for teenagers when she was in high school and it was reported still to be one.

Harriet had been reported as possibly having been

raped pending a coroner's examination. Her murder remained unsolved. She was unmarried but was known to have been dating several members of the class frequently; as well as a local doctor, Henry Calio.

Dr Calio was in Orlando Florida attending a medical convention when Harriet's body was found. He was not a suspect in the murder because Harriet had been seen at a baby shower on June 19th held for Mary Ann Hitchens, a classmate and close friend. The party was held at the Seaford Golf and Country Club.

Mary Ann was expecting her first child in August, and Dr. Calio left for Florida on June 17th two days before the baby shower where Harriet was last seen.

The reunion was held on June 22nd the day after she was found murdered. Dr. Calio was in still in Orlando on the date of the shower and was still in Florida when the body was found. The Coroner determined that Harriet had been murdered the night of the baby shower on June 17th.

Harriet's death was the topic of discussion by those attending the reunion. Why she was murdered was a mystery and it was the general opinion of those attending, that the murderer had to be someone that picked her up after she left the baby shower. All the ladies at the shower where she was last seen were very close friends.

The police had interviewed everyone who was at the shower individually. They all reported that Harriet left the party alone and most of those interviewed added that she was driving her new red convertible and that its convertible top was down even though it was dark. One of the persons attending the party stated that Harriet had mentioned to her that she had to stop at the deli to pick up a few items.

The police had eliminated everyone at the party as being a suspect. Three different women attending the party stated that they had seen Harriet as she left the party and that she was driving and alone in her own automobile.

Harriet's parents, with whom she lived, told the police the following morning that she failed to come home from the shower and a search was started. Two boys found her body as they prepared to put a canoe in the Nanticoke River from a clearing on The Island.

Marlene Martin, a local woman, after reading of the murder in the Wilmington Morning News that Harriet was reported to have been last seen at a party, called the police, and told the detective working on the case, that she had seen Harriet at the Central Avenue Deli Market the night of the baby shower, and she saw a tall white man talking to her in the Deli's parking lot.

She told detective Jack Truitt, that Harriet was sitting alone in her automobile, a red convertible.

"When I waved to Harriet she recognized me and returned the wave. I did not recognize or see the man's face that Harriet was talking too as he had his back to me."

"Harriet must have known the man because their conversation was lengthy. Harriet was talking to the man when I went in the deli and she was still talking to him when I returned to my own car parked next to Harriet's."

When asked, she told the detective the convertible top was down on the car, and she had a clear view of Harriet.

"The man Harriet was talking to was standing outside Harriet's car and Harriet was sitting behind the steering wheel in the car talking to him. He was a tall and thin, well dressed white man, who had his back to me, he was bending over talking to Harriet seated in the car on the driver's side but I did not recognize him or see his face. I don't know if she had already been in the deli or not."

The owner of the Central Avenue Deli said he remembered Harriet coming into the market and that she had bought a few grocery items. He felt certain that she was alone.

He added that she was a regular customer at the deli and she almost always bought four bananas. He knew her and her parents well. He remembered asking Harriet if she was going to her class reunion that she had been telling him about and he said she had told him she would definitely be going.

When the deli owner was told about his customer's remarks, he said that he had not seen Harriet talking to anyone outside the deli and he could not recall any particular men that may have been in the deli before or after she was there.

Harriet's car was found abandoned in Laurel, Delaware

just about seven miles south of Seaford parked in the Centenary Methodist Church parking lot off of West Street. No fingerprints were found on the car including the steering wheel.

The police assumed the vehicle had been wiped clean by someone, but Harriet's own fingerprints were found on several of the items still in the grocery bag on the floor behind the driver's seat. Several other prints, found on the contents in the grocery bag, proved to be that of the deli owner.

The keys to the car were not found, and there was no money or credit cards in her purse found on the front seat. It was the open empty purse lying on the seat that caused the sexton of the church to call the Laurel police when he realized the car had been there over night. The convertible's top was up.

The Seaford police added robbery to the charges that would be charged to the murderer when he was apprehended.

The grocery bag contained a quart of melted ice cream, a quart of warm milk, and four bananas. Detective Truitt reported that she would have gone home with those items before going to Laurel and theorized she may have been forced to drive the car to Laurel, or the car may have been stolen.

The reunion was held at the Flagship Restaurant, a former working boat that had been permanently attached and anchored to a concrete dock off the Nanticoke River, and converted into a restaurant and bar.

The Flagship was famous for both its atmosphere as well as its food. It had a small dance floor on an exterior dock facing the river. The small dance floor on the dock floor was surrounded by tables and chairs. Local musicians played there regularly on Saturday nights and on special occasions such as the reunion. It was one of the few spots in the Seaford area where live music, food, and drinks were served.

Following the reunion dinner, all in attendance were introduced and asked to give their fellow classmates a few words about themselves including their marriage status, number of children, their place of employment, their place of residence, and anything special that they had done or seen over the past five years.

Edward Morgan reported that he had just returned from a trip to Israel and had been to Jerusalem while there. He stated it was a trip that he would never forget.

John Smith stated that he had become the father of triplets and was Pampers best customer.

Irene Wallace stated that her husband William, had been selected to be the Pastor of the First Baptist Church in Onancock, Virginia and they would be moving to Onancock in the following week.

Fred McGee who was always the class comedian reported that he still held the record for stacking the most beer cans in a pyramid triangle. "I tried to beat my old record but when I tried to remove one of the cans when I found it was not empty, the whole darn thing fell down."

President, William Grogan gave a report for those members not attending the reunion but had sent in a brief copy of their activities over the past five years to Grace Smith, the reunion secretary.

Following the introductions a eulogy was presented in memory of Harriet O'Brien by Ida Smoot and several of her classmates including a teary eyed personal eulogy by Jeanne Records that had all in attendance in tears.

After Jeanne's eulogy the official business of the reunion was closed with a prayer by Irene Wallace's husband, and the bar was opened and music began playing. Many of the members remained on the Flagship for the remainder of the evening, dancing and in conversation that consisted mostly of memories of the past. The talk got a little louder as the evening passed and after a few drinks. By 11:30 pm the last of the classmates had departed for home.

During the evening following dinner, there was a lot of discussion on the fact that Horace Hastings and his wife Helen were both at the reunion and were not together. It was well known Horace and Helen had been separated for over a year.

Horace came to the reunion alone; but his wife Helen, came with another man. She and this stranger did not dance all evening, but Helen did dance with two or three of her classmates over the course of the evening when she was asked.

Horace was dancing with many of the ladies and was drinking quite heavily. Most of his dances were with Jeanne Records.

The ladies were all shocked to see that Helen had brought a man as her guest to the reunion while her divorce was still in the courts. The ladies were also very upset when she failed to introduce him to any of them when they dropped by Helen's table to talk.

He was simply introduced as a 'friend of mine from Salisbury, Maryland'. Gossip soon had him identified most likely as her suitor from Salisbury, Maryland.

In apparent retribution, Horace was busy dancing with most every single woman at the reunion and a few married ladies as well. He was indeed the life of the party. Because he danced with Jeanne Records so many times over the evening, all the ladies were discussing the possibility that he and Jeanne just might get together after Horace's divorce was finalized. Jeanne had invited a friend Toby Foster, to the reunion but was almost ignoring him.

Jeanne and Toby left the reunion together shortly after Horace left as the party was breaking up. Helen and her guest had left at least an hour earlier.

On June 24th two days following the reunion, the almost nude body of Jeanne Records was found in a marsh just off the Nanticoke River by two fishermen. An autopsy revealed that she had been strangled by a length of what appeared to be a small wire cable of some sort which was still wrapped around her neck.

The marks on Jeanne's neck were compared with the marks found on Harriet and it was the opinion of the Forensic team, that the marks on Harriet's neck were identical to those on Jeanne and that they most likely were caused by the same wire cable.

The wire or cable used to strangle Harriet was not found at the area where Harriet's body was found and it was also the general opinion of the investigating team that the same wire may have been used on both women and that both women had been murdered by the same person.

The Coroner's report however, stated Jeanne had definitely been raped. Her body had multiple bruises and small lacerations and there was human skin under her fingernails from which a DNA sample was taken. It was evident that she had fought her attacker. In contrast, Harriet's body had no signs of abuse and she was fully clothed.

Jeanne was another member of the school cheerleaders and girls basketball team. Like Harriet, she had been strangled in the same manner as Harriet.

The Coroner reported that both ladies had been strangled with a length of a small wire around the neck. His earlier examination of Harriet, to determine if she had been raped, was questionable, because there were no signs of abuse on her body and her clothes had no signs of a struggle.

The report did confirm that she had recent sexual activity and that she was in the early months of a pregnancy.

Jeanne's guest at the reunion Toby Foster, was not a member of the class and had moved to Seaford a little over two years ago. He was a supervisor at the local duPont Nylon plant and had transferred from the engineering office of that company located in Newark, Delaware.

Jeanne was also an employee of the nylon plant and it was at work where she had met Toby. They were dating frequently; but there had been no mention of an engagement or of any marriage plans.

Toby was interviewed by Lieutenant Jack Truitt of the Seaford Police department, and Toby told Jack that he had not seen Jeanne since the night of her class reunion. He was very upset over her death and told the detective that he had planned to give her an engagement ring for her birthday on July 12th.

Toby was asked about a report they had regarding Jeanne's dancing so many times with Horace Hastings at the reunion. They asked if he was offended by her doing that. He told Jack that Jeanne and Horace were very good friends and because of Horace's being so embarrassed by his estranged wife's bringing a man to the reunion, that she wanted to cheer Horace up.

Toby said that Jeanne also needed to be cheered up because she was emotionally upset herself because Harriet had been her best friend since high school days. "I don't like dancing that much anyway."

"We had dinner the next evening at Monaco's Restaurant."

"You said we -- who were the 'we' that you had dinner with Toby?"

"Oh sorry, it was just Jeanne, and I."

"I thought you said you said you had not seen her since the night of the reunion?"

"Yes, I did say that didn't I? I guess I forgot that until you asked me about Horace dancing so much with Jeanne. I must admit I was a little concerned about her doing that, until she explained to me over dinner of her close friendship with both Horace and Jeanne. She knew that I was concerned about the way she treated me at the party and asked me to have dinner with her so she could explain."

"She explained that Horace was just a close friend and that she was so upset over Harriet's death. She told me that she was talking more with Horace, about Harriet's possible murderer, than she was dancing. She explained to me that when they were on the dance floor was the only way they could discuss the subject without an audience."

"Did she tell you any of the thoughts she or Horace had on the death of Harriet?"

"As a matter of fact she did. She mentioned to me that Horace had told her that Harriet thought she was pregnant."

"Did Harriet say who the father was?"

"No, I asked Jeanne that very same question myself and Jeanne told me that Harriet refused to tell her, but she did say that Harriet was going to marry the man soon."

"Jeanne also told me that she wondered if the father was the person who killed Harriet. Perhaps he may not have wanted to get married or to pay child support."

"Did she mention what Horace's thoughts were on the killing of Harriet?"

"Jeanne did tell me that Horace was very upset because he and Harriet had been close friends since high school days and that he was not surprised about the pregnancy because she was dating so many men and some of them were rather questionable. He thought that it was probably one of them."

"Wonder what he meant by questionable?"

"I'm not sure Horace told her that exact word, I used that word simply to mean that Jeanne told me that she certainly would have never dated many of them."

"Did Jeanne give you any names that Harriet had dated recently?"

"No, but I do know a few of them I have seen her with, let's see, There was Dr. Calio, She was dating him a lot. Then there is a man named Douglas, but I don't know his last name, Oh yes, there was a man from Georgetown, who Jeanne told me impregnated a girl in her class at her high school. I told Jeanne he would be one that I would question."

"She said his parents paid a lot of money to settle that situation. I have seen him several times with Harriet at the Flagship Restaurant. He was a heavy drinker like Horace. He was loud when he was drinking, but I have never seen him really get out of the way. He just gets mouthy."

"He was what I call a 'hugger'. He was always hugging every pretty woman he saw. In my opinion, he thought he was God's gift to women, but most of the women found him obnoxious. Jeanne didn't like him because he knocked up a high school friend of hers and then wouldn't marry her."

"What was that girl's name?"

"I really don't know and if Jeanne gave me her name I don't remember it. I wasn't living in Seaford at that time."

"There were other men dating Harriet, but because I have only been in Seaford for the past two years, I just don't know all of their names yet."

The Wilmington Morning News and the Salisbury Times reported in their newspapers the next morning, that the police had a report of a man who was seen talking to Harriet outside the Central Street Deli Market, but he had not yet been identified. The case remained open and was still under investigation.

The case of Jeanne Records' murder was also reported as under investigation and that both the girls were thought to have been murdered by the same individual.

TWO

ROY TULL AND Carl McAllister were having lunch at the Spot Diner a few days after Jeanne's body was found.

Roy asked, "Carl, have you given any thought to the fact that both of the murdered women were in our graduation class and that they were murdered since or before our class reunion?"

"Harriet was killed just before the reunion and now Jeanne was murdered following the reunion. Could they have been raped and murdered by one of our own classmates?"

Carl replied, "Yes, but I wouldn't bet on that. I think it may have been a complete stranger who is a sex offender that just happened to be in Seaford at the time of our reunion. But to be honest Roy, a few of us were talking about the possibility of the killer being a classmate last evening at the Lions Club meeting."

"If this keeps up, we will have no one coming to our next reunion. I sure hope that they find the killer or killers soon."

"If the same person did both the killings, as the newspaper stated was the case, and they were both raped as the paper suggested; it looks like we may have a rapist on the loose here in Seaford. I know that my wife won't go out at all after dark."

"Mine won't either. I think that being both women were in the same class at school, the killer must have known both of them pretty well and used his identity to get with them. Perhaps, he might be one of our own classmates, but doesn't live in the Seaford area."

"I don't know about that; but I think we should talk to Chief of Police Daley, to see if he is aware that both the girls were in the same class and both girls were killed just before or after having attended the reunion. Maybe there is a connection that just may lead them to the killer."

"I agree with that Roy. I will talk to him about those thoughts later today after I get my men working on the job. It just may be a possibility that the police could follow up on"

" If I recall correctly both girls were always the best of friends, and I sure can't think of a reason as to why anyone would want to kill either of them so it may be as you mentioned, just a sex offender who just happened to be in Seaford at the time of the reunion."

"I think you're right; but if that's the case, he hung around town for at least several days, because the murders were two or three days apart weren't they? Maybe they can check the motel records or determine if there were any strangers hanging around here somewhere."

"Of course it could also be a local man; but why all of a sudden does he start raping ladies? I can't ever remember of a girl or woman being raped around here. Do you?"

"Not recently anyway, but come to think of it, I think that there was talk of a rape when we were in high school. Can you remember anything like that?"

"Now that you mention it, wasn't there talk about Kathy Black being raped in our senior year?"

"Yes; but it was all talk because if I remember correctly, she denied being raped and finally quit school and left Seaford to marry a guy from down south somewhere. Robert Miller, if you remember him, had been dating her all the way through high school and he was devastated when she ran off with someone else. That is what prompted the talk about her being raped."

"Yes I do remember Robert and all the talk about that; but Kathy came back to Seaford and now works at the library. She told me that she had married after she left Seaford and was now divorced. She has a little boy."

Later that afternoon, Carl stopped by the police station and asked to talk to the Chief of Police. The chief, Richard Daley was told of Carl's request to talk with him about the two murders and Carl was told that the chief would see him right away.

"Chief, we have some information that may have a bearing on the murders of Harriet O'Brien and Jeanne Records. We have nothing that proves our thoughts, but we think that we should at least tell you what we were discussing relative to those two murders."

"Who are the 'we' you mention Carl?"

"Oh yes, I should have said Roy Tull and I were discussing the murders and the question came up as to whether there could be a connection between the two murders and our class reunion."

"Both girls were members of our graduation class of 1984 and both murders were evidently committed just after or before our class reunion. We just thought that was not a coincidence and wonder if there could be a connection."

"Well Carl, we were unaware that they were classmates or knew each other; but we do think that they were both murdered by the same person. I thank you for bringing this to my attention and we will keep that thought in our investigation."

"Now a question for you Carl, can you remember any strangers that were at your reunion? You did go yourself didn't you?"

"Yes, I was there chief, and come to think of it there were several strangers there. Most were husbands or wives of a classmate. A few strangers were there with a classmate. I am pretty sure that if you contract Grace Smith, she will have the record of everyone who came and those who did not come."

"Who is the Grace Smith do you mean Carl?"

"She is the person who maintains the mailing list of our class members and of those who came or did not come. Grace married Franklin Smith, you know him, he has a plumbing business on Front Street."

"Yes, I know both Grace and Frank. I will be in contact with her. I think that we will also be contacting all the class members to see if we can come up with a reason why these women were murdered and raped, even though it is questionable, whether one of the women had been raped. We will not limit our search for a sex offender or rapist but anyone that may have had a reason to kill them."

The chief's phone rang and he was told that another body, a young man, had just been found in the marsh east of Seaford off the Nanticoke River by two men who were training their beagle hounds to chase rabbits. The body had been snagged by a fallen tree limb that prevented it from floating out into the river at a high tide. This was the same general area where the two women were found.

"Carl, you will have to excuse me, I have just been advised that another body has been found near the Nanticoke River in a marsh. I must get out there right away. I will be in touch with you later."

"Oh dear lord, I understand Chief; did they tell you if the woman has been identified yet? I do hope it was not another one of our classmates."

"No the body has not been identified yet; but Carl,

this one is not a women, it is a young man. Sorry, I have to go now. I will be in touch."

The body was soon identified as being that of Horace Hastings, another member of the class of 1984. Horace was a wealthy farmer and owned broiler houses that produced a total of 20,000 broiler size chickens for the market every week of the year. The farm operation was a family business but Horace had created his own totally owned poultry operation.

His two brothers and his father were active in separate farm operations. They provided Horace with a large portion of the poultry feed required for his poultry operation after it was processed at a nearby feed plant. Horace owned a ten percent stake in the feed mill.

Horace was married and had two children, a boy of three and a daughter of four. When in school he was a star football player. His wife Helen Groton was in his high school graduating class. They were married during their junior year at The University of Delaware. He and Helen both graduated from the University in 1988.

He had been shot in the back of his head. When found, his wallet contained a total of $163.00 and there was no evidence of his being robbed. A 32 caliber pistol and a spent bullet casing were found near the body. The scene had the appearance of a suicide.

The Forensic investigators; however, noted in their report that the body was not thought to have been shot where it was found, because there was no blood on the leaves or the ground near the body and there was no evidence of a robbery, because his wallet contained a larger than usual amount of cash and no credit cards were taken.

The team had also concluded that there were indications the body had been dragged from the dirt road just off the highway. Detective Truitt said, "It is apparent that someone had attempted to make the killing look like a suicide, but he surely didn't do a very good job of doing so."

The newspaper headlines the next morning read that a third member of the Seaford High School Class of 1984 had been found in a river and he had been shot. All of which included a rehash of the women being raped and murdered. They now added information to their feature story that all three of the victims had been attending a reunion of their high school class.

The paper should have read two of them attended the reunion, because Harriet was killed the day before the reunion. Chief Daley had his secretary call them about the error.

Later in the same day, Horace's automobile was found parked at Jimmy's restaurant which was a favorite stop for the locals for a quick sandwich, a coffee break, and was the local gossip center, especially in the morning hours. The owner of the restaurant, Jimmy Johnson, had recognized the automobile as belonging to Horace and promptly called the police after hearing of Horace's murder or suicide.

Jack Truitt, a detective with the Seaford police

department and assigned to head the investigations of the three murders was asked to determine if anyone at the restaurant had remembered seeing Horace.

Jack was told by Chief Daley that he had requested assistance from the FBI because it was possible a serial killer may have been responsible for the multiple killings, but he would still be the head of the team. He said he would release that at a press interview scheduled later that afternoon.

Now that a man had been killed, the previous thought that the killer was a sex predator was no longer the suspected prime motive.

The Coroner filed his report after the autopsy and with the report of the Forensic team, the Chief of Police was told that Horace was definitely murdered and it was not a suicide. Apparently the killer attempted to set the scene to appear as a suicide; but he had made a terrible error, by placing a 32 caliber pistol and shell casing near the body when, he was actually shot with a 45 caliber bullet.

Jack, said, "He must not watch many movies or TV, everyone knows that there is always a Coroner's autopsy and investigation after any mysterious death."

The fact that this was the second member of the high school class attending the reunion and the third had registered to attend but was killed just before the reunion, caused the investigators to focus their interviews with the members of the class for a possible motive.

The newspapers had picked up the connections and

started referring to the murders as The Class Reunion Murders.

Chief Daley called a meeting of the department's investigating team, to review what had been obtained to this point.

He told the team. "I will announce this afternoon at an interview with the press that I have requested the assistance of the FBI because we are concerned that there is a possibility a serial killer is involved with the murders, and the FBI has already asked that we prepare a report of just what we have found so far, what we have planned, and our opinions on the murders. So we need to get started on that for them."

"I have requested their assistance and they have agreed to assist us in solving the cases we have. Jack Truitt will still head our team."

A summary list was prepared from the transcripts already on file. It included in the case of Horace's death that robbery had already been eliminated as a motive. Horace had a large sum of money on his body when found.

In the case of Harriet, it appeared that she had been robbed, but the police felt that the appearance of a robbery had actually been staged because of the manner in which her purse and contents were laid out on the front seat of her car in clear view. There were no fingerprints on anything in Harriet's car except on a shopping bag and its contents. Her credit cards and cash were taken from her wallet but as yet her cards had not been used since her death. They were confident that the car had been wiped clean and parked at the church lot to appear as if there was a robbery. There was also no attempt to hide the car where it would not be found so quickly.

Detective Truitt added remarks that he was sure Harriet didn't drive that car to Laurel voluntarily. She surely would have taken the ice cream and milk home before going to Laurel unless she was forced to do so. He stated that he had found no reason as to why she would have gone to Laurel late in the evening after having attended a baby shower.

Being her body was found in Seaford, it is my opinion, that the killer killed Harriet, probably in Seaford, and took her car to Laurel and abandoned it merely to make it appear as a hijacking and robbery by someone.

The report stated-- Perhaps he lives in Laurel; but if he killed her to steal her car why did he take it only to Laurel, a distance of less than ten miles? We find it hard to believe that he would kill for a ride home and whatever cash she may have had with her. We think he is trying to confuse us as to his motive.

We have as yet not uncovered anything that helps us with the murder of Jeanne Records. She was definitely thought to have been raped.

Our plan at the moment is to continue with our investigations. We will interview those class members that now live in Laurel but we are almost positive the killer does not live in Laurel. We feel that no one could be stupid enough to rob and kill someone and park the stolen car in his own hometown the size of Laurel, where everyone knows most everyone in town.

Our job is to determine just what the motive behind these murders could be. We are concerned as to why all the victims are members of the class of 84.

After the Wilmington Branch Office of the FBI received Chief Daley's request for assistance and the summary of the events that the team had prepared, agent William Carle read the summary report sent to them as well as copies of all the actual interview transcripts and recognized the names of Horace Hastings and Helen Groton.

They were persons known to him. They were among his college classmates at the University of Delaware and he knew personally. He had himself dated Helen Groton in her freshman and sophomore years at Delaware. He then asked permission of the branch manager to take the case.

His request was approved and he and agent Bob Spedden were advised to report to the police chief, Richard Daley, in Seaford Delaware on Monday of the following week.

When agent Carle read that the third victim was Horace Hastings, he immediately called Horace's widow Helen on the telephone to offer her his condolences. He told Helen who he was and asked if she remembered him from their days at the University of Delaware.

She replied, "How could I ever forget you Bill. Those were wonderful days. Where are you now?"

He advised her, "I am with the FBI, Helen, and believe it or not, I have been assigned to the case involving the death of Horace and those two other classmates of yours."

"Oh great, we do need help."

"I will be in Seaford Monday morning, and I would like to get together with you as soon as possible. Perhaps we could have dinner somewhere where we could reminisce on our old college days and also discuss this terrible thing that will bring me downstate."

"That would be wonderful Bill, I really would like to see you again, and I do need a trusted friend to give me some assistance in handling this situation. I have a lot to tell you. Just give me a call when you get down here and I will be glad to have dinner with you. Perhaps even a drink. Let's see, I think it's manhattans that you like."

"Yes, that's right you've got a good memory. I will see you Monday afternoon."

Chief Daley summoned his team to the conference room immediately after the two FBI agents detailed to him arrived in Seaford.

Chief Daley announced again that Jack Truitt would head up the Police Department's team investigation and he then introduced the two FBI agents, William Carle and Robert Spedden and then told the team that they were to assist the agents in any way when asked, and that he in turn had been promised the full cooperation and services of the FBI. They have advised me that Agent Carle would be the FBI leader in their investigation.

Agent Carle then assumed the podium and led the discussions on the murders and the procedure to be taken to determine the motives for the killings that would lead to finding the guilty party.

"You are to direct your operations with the belief that a classmate may be the murderer and your task is to find the motive for the killings; but we do not know for certain that the murderer was a member of the class."

"Now that a man has been killed, it is apparent that there is more to the case then rape and robbery as we first suspected. That is apparent because Mr. Hastings had a large sum of money in his wallet when he was found and the Coroner thinks that only Miss Records was raped. It is very possible that the killer is directing his actions against members of the graduating class of 1984. We are offered a challenge to determine if that is true, and just what his motive is."

"The FBI records, where we were called into the case, indicate that we have had several instances in the past where college alumni members got together and renewed long standing differences that ended in criminal activity; but the records indicate that we have never experienced a murder at one, and that we have never had any cases involving a problem at a high school reunion."

"Don't let the feeling we have at the moment -- that, we think these murders were committed by a fellow classmate -- become public knowledge just now, especially to the class members themselves."

"We don't want to frighten those members of the

class, although I know that several of the members have already approached your Chief on that possibility. We don't want to add anything to increase their anxiety to the point that they will be afraid to answer our questions. We need to keep them talking."

Agent Bill Carle then told the team that he had a personal interest in the case because he knew Horace Hastings and his wife Helen from his days at the University of Delaware.

"I have an appointment to meet with Mrs. Hastings this afternoon and agent Bob Spedden will be meeting with the parents of the two ladies who were murdered. We want them to know that we are here to find the killer of their daughters or in Mrs. Hastings' case her husband."

"What I would like for all of you to do first is to start interviewing all the members of the class, discreetly, to see if we can find any motives. Look for jealousy, sex orientation, hatred, money, or anything that could possibly stir enough hatred in someone to cause him to kill three different people."

"As I said awhile ago, agent Spedden and I will start our investigation with Mrs. Hastings, and the parents of the two women who were murdered. It is important that the families of the victims are made aware that we are working hard to find the killers and at the same time we will determine if they themselves have any thoughts on why their loved ones were killed."

"I am happy that Chief Daley has ordered a DNA markup on both women and hopefully that may positively confirm that both of them were killed by the same person and in time may identify the murderer for us, or at least determine who or who did not rape Jeanne Records."

"As you know a court approved DNA report takes about two to four months to get an opinion; so in the meantime, we will assume the rape and murders were all by the same man. Why there has now been a man killed, is at present, a mystery to us. In reviewing what information we already have, we have concluded that just perhaps Horace may have known or discovered who the murderer was."

"Direct your questions to the class members, to questions primarily about the three that have been killed. Write these questions down to ask all the members."

"1 - Did either of the victims have dates or friendships with anyone that went sour?"

"2 - Do they recall any threats having been made in high school or recently against any of the three?"

"3 -When and where was the last time they saw any of them?"

"4 - We need to check on the description of the only suspect we have at the moment and determine if any classmate fits into that description. The one suspect described by the woman at the deli claims a tall white man was seen talking with the first girl that was killed, Harriet O'Brien. Who in the class is tall?"

"We need to know who that man was. He was reported as being a tall white man and that is all we have on him. I feel he is a strong suspect. Let's look closely at all the tall members of the class."

"We also need to talk with Toby Foster, who is listed at this time as the last person to have dated Jeanne Records. She took him to the reunion as a guest."

"5 - Has anyone mentioned seeing her after the night of the reunion?"

"6 – What do they know about Robert Miller, did they talk with him?

Detective Truitt interrupted, "Mr. Carle, I have an appointment to talk with Jimmy Johnson this afternoon at 3:00 to see if anyone at his restaurant, where Horace's car was found, can recall any helpful leads. I have a feeling that Horace knew the person he rode off with and of course never came back to get his car."

"Jack please call me Bill, I want you all to think of Bob and I simply as members of your own team. Yes, I think working on Mr. Hastings death is a very good place to start."

"Ok Bill, we also have a witness who is thought to be the last to see Harriet alive; and she told us that Harriet was talking to someone -- again a tall white man as reported to us by a witness who also said that Harriett acted as if she knew him. I have a feeling it is one and the same person."

Agent Carle again broke in and said, "I think that we should start checking the backgrounds on everyone in the class especially the tall men."

Chief Daley interrupted, "Yes Bill, I understand that is

already underway and I should have the first reports later today but one thing that I have almost always found that has to be answered in the very beginning, involving the murder of a family member, is to determine the possibility that the spouse or a family member is involved, especially if there is money involved or if there are marital problems. Will you be investigating those possibilities?"

"Absolutely Chief you are correct in that assumption. As I mentioned earlier, I have already scheduled a meeting with Mrs. Hastings this afternoon, and while I will be renewing an old relationship with her, by having dinner with her this evening, my purpose will be to determine if there is a possibility that she had anything to do with her husband's murder."

"You are correct in your statement that in the majority of murders of a spouse, family members are the most likely to be guilty because they usually have the most to gain. In the case of Mrs. Hastings, she and her husband were having marital problems and we will certainly keep that in mind."

After the meeting was over, agent Carle called Horace's widow, Helen Hastings, and arranged to meet her in the afternoon at her home as he had arranged by telephone before he came down to Seaford.

THREE

HELEN WAS WAITING for his arrival and greeted him with a hug and began crying. "Oh Bill, you don't know how happy I am to see you. I need a strong shoulder to cry on. You don't know how bad things have been going for me lately."

"Helen, I'm happy to see you too and I do wish it could have been on different circumstances. It's been quite awhile since we were at the university hasn't it?"

"Yes, seven years to be exact Bill. You left, if I remember correctly, in the start of my junior year. If you had not left, I may not have been in this mess today."

"Why did my leaving the university have any bearing on the situation?"

"Well, when you were in Delaware, I was dating you, not Horace, if you will remember."

"That's right, I thought of that myself when I read

the case transcript. We were getting somewhat serious weren't we?"

"Yes we were, I was brokenhearted when you transferred to Tennessee. I cried for a month. The distance apart finished it for us didn't it? I haven't heard from you since you last called me from Tennessee the following Christmas eve. I didn't know that you had joined the FBI, when did you do that?"

"I made an application for the position shortly after I got my master's degree, and was lucky enough to have been selected. I was first assigned to the office in Nashville, but when I saw an opening in Delaware last year, I decided to seek a transfer to be closer to the ocean and to the beaches. That too worked out as I wanted. I did love the fun we all used to have at both Rehoboth Beach and at Ocean City. In Tennessee I really missed the weekends at the beach. Do you remember the bonfire parties we used to have on Coin Road?"

"Yes, especially those nights on Coin Road. Those were fun days Bill. I am so happy that you are here. You sure haven't changed too much. I feel like the entire world is sitting on my shoulders. Tell me did you marry that girl you had met and told me about in Tennessee?"

"No, Helen that just didn't work out at all. I'm still single and my job with the bureau now makes it very difficult for any kind of social life anymore. I understand that you and Horace have two children."

"Yes, that's right a boy and a girl. I don't know how much of my many problems you know about; but Horace and I have been separated for almost two years now and we were in the midst of a divorce when all of this happened. We still lived under the same roof because of the children; but that was all."

"He seldom came home except to pick up clothes or things from his office. When he came to check on the broiler houses every day he periodically made a point to see the children and he always asked me if there was anything I needed. He never abused me or argued in front of the children. We knew that our differences were irreconcilable."

"Helen, do you feel like talking to me about all that just now. I have to get some answers to help us get to the bottom of these murders. But we can wait until after dinner this evening if you like,"

"Yes, I understand Bill. I want it all to end soon. I am happy to answer anything you need to know and the sooner the better for me. First let me tell you about Horace and me. Perhaps that will answer some of the questions I know you will have to have me answer."

"Horace as you probably already know had become very successful. My parents loaned us $50,000 to build two new broiler houses just after we were married and we were at the very beginning of the then booming broiler business using large capacity production techniques. That loan and two large bank loans that my father signed for us got us started in a big way."

"We have 20,000 broilers going to market every week out of our two buildings. Each building has two floors of seven partitioned areas. His college studies taught him that chicks will eat 24 hours a day if it does not get dark. Horace placed automatic watering and feeding systems in each house and installed overhead lights and fans that we turn off only on the one free section of each house that is being sanitized and cleaned each week after the broilers are sold in preparation for the next 20,000 baby chicks, "biddies" as we call them."

"Each section has chicks one week older than the previous section. They eat constantly and become broiler size much earlier than in the past. So we have marketable broilers ready for the market almost every week from different sections of the two story buildings. Each section was originally filled with biddies a week apart, and that now gives us ongoing marketable broilers. Our broilers are actually sold the day we put them in the houses as biddies."

"Most growers, including us, have contracts with the hatcheries and feed companies to sell them at set prices when they are placed in our houses. We use for the most part, our own feed, which is grown on our family farms. The feed company processes our crops for us so our contract is usually only with a food processor such as Perdue. We buy our own baby chicks from the local Hatchery."

"Needless to say, Horace got in the business at the right time, and we have accumulated a very substantial financial position. But that success is when our troubles started, once Horace became so well off, he changed completely.

When the large broiler houses started producing such large numbers, a lot of small time broiler farmers were put out of business because they could not produce broilers as quick or as cheap as the new automatic houses."

"When Horace was murdered, it was my first thought that perhaps one of those farmers may have been the murderer, but I then realized that was not the case. None of his friends ever held anything against Horace and many of them were helped by Horace at times when they were changing their farm operations. Then I realized that they would not be involved with killing the women and that the murders were probably by a single killer as the police suggest."

"Horace started associating with big time growers more and more, and many of his old farmer friends quit long time friendships with him, because they could not afford Horace's new lifestyle. Horace even bought a very expensive yacht that he keeps at the Indian River Inlet off the ocean. I hated that life style. All the men do now is drink and mess with their boats. If he did not have a good man like Steve Cockran looking out for his poultry business, I'm sure it would all soon go to pot. I quit going down to the boat a long time ago."

"All he worried about was making more money. He started associating with money people and created friendships with many of them. He was doing a lot of drinking and was away from home with his new found friends mostly in the evenings and almost every weekend.

He was always late getting home and always told me that he was on business."

"About two years ago after he bought the yacht he began spending weekends boating and partying on it with his new friends. That was when he quit making love with me; and it was then that I suspected he was having an affair with someone. I approached him on that and he told me that he was entertaining business associates and was not having an affair. That is also when he told me he just didn't love me anymore. He said I was no fun and he was enjoying his boating and his new friends, adding that he was going to divorce me."

"I told him that he didn't have to do that because I was going to file for a divorce myself and I was going to see to it that he would have to split the assets of the business with me because it was my parent's money that created the business for his start. Of course he said no way. He offered to pay me $200,000 over four years which I refused."

"I told him that I wanted full time custody of our two children. I didn't want them to be exposed to Horace's new life style. I was hoping that I could prove adultery and felt that would help my case. He would not agree to those two items and that is where we stood at the time of his death."

"I think I would have agreed to a compromise on the money, if he would have agreed to my total custody of the children, but Larry, the man that was advising me on my divorce told me not to do so until we had to do that."

"For the past three or four months, it has been one accusation after another, as his lawyer attempted to have me agree to a settlement that I just didn't feel was fair. I have two children to bring up and educate and his success is the direct result of my parent's money not his own doing. His lawyer even told me that I would probably be the heir to my parent's estate as an only child and I didn't need to destroy Horace's business. That really made me mad."

"Then to protect my interests, I was introduced to a businessman from Salisbury, Maryland, Larry Adams, that I mentioned a minute or so ago, who was recommended to me as someone who could make sure that I was not making any bad decisions."

"I even took him to our class reunion hoping to catch some pictures of Horace flirting and hugging all over the women at the reunion so that we could claim adultery and infidelity. Larry said that would make the judge settle in my favor."

"I understand that since I was seen with Larry all kinds, of claims of my infidelity have been spread by Horace. Bill, regardless of what you may have heard or may soon hear, I have no interest in that man and I have had no personal relations with him or anyone. I have no desire to do so."

"I believe you Helen, and after I dig into these cases, I will probably have more questions for you. So the only questions I have for you at the moment are, if you have any thoughts on who could have killed Horace other than a farmer who was forced out of the poultry business?"

"No I can't think or comprehend anyone capable of doing that."

"Did anyone owe him any money that you are aware of?"

"Not that I am aware of. He does loan our farm manager, Steve Cockran a few dollars every so often until payday, but certainly never enough to cause a murder. I do know that he went on a note for one of his friends to build a house similar to ours but not as big. But that note was paid off a long time ago. Horace was always ready to help his farmer friends."

"If he was having an affair with another woman, do you know who she was, and if you think that someone may have been upset about that, like a disgruntled husband, or another man?"

"I have no proof of anyone with whom he was actually having an affair or who may have owed him money. I have been told by friends that he was playing the field just as he always did in high school."

"I always suspected it was either Jeanne Records or Harriet O'Brien; they were always after him in school. My friends just won't give me any clue. I do know that many of his old school pals are jealous of his success. The only thing that comes to my mind is if someone used the death of the two girls, to make it look like their murderer was also the one that killed Horace. Does that seem logical to you that there just might be two murderers?"

"Yes, that is a possibility, but we still need to know who would benefit by Horace's death."

"Well that sure puts me in top position doesn't it?"

"Well perhaps, we will get some of the answers to all the motives soon and see if we can come up with a few suspects. How about our dinner this evening, any special place you like?"

"Well most of my friends go to the Flagship, but I would just as soon go somewhere else until all this mess blows over."

"Okay, I got an idea, how about riding down to Rehoboth Beach? I am anxious to see the place again."

"I would love that Bill. That will bring back a lot of memories. I do remember the many bonfires we all went to together on Coin Road? I will call my babysitter, I'm sure she will be available. What time?"

"Great, I'll pick you up at 5:00 if that is Ok? Yes I do remember those great times with the hamburgers, hotdogs, beer, and of course the snuggling."

"Then 5:00 it is. My nosey neighbors will have something else to talk about for a change. But of course there will be no snuggling on Coin Road."

Detective Jack Truitt and agent Bob Spedden arrived at Jimmy's restaurant promptly at 3:00 and sat at a booth with the owner Jimmy Johnson. They all had a cup of coffee to sip on. The detective said, "Jimmy thanks for calling us about Horace's car being parked in your parking lot. Do you recall if Horace came in the restaurant that day or was it the day before?"

"Yes Jack, Horace stops by almost every day and it was usually about the same time, about 8:30 in the morning, there is a gang of men who do that regularly for coffee and breakfast."

"I am positive that he came in the restaurant in the morning of the day before he was found murdered. he told me that he was looking for a couple of men to clean his broiler houses and he asked me to tell anyone who might like a steady job to contact him. I remember him saying it's a dirty job, but a full time job never the less and that he would give me a poster the next day to post for him. He never came in the next day with the poster and that was the day we found his car."

"I just can't recall his being with anyone or the exact time he left. In fact, I didn't notice his car was still in the lot until Steve Willis asked me why Horace had left his car there overnight, when he came in the next morning."

"Steve told me that it was parked there the night before when he came home from a meeting of the amateur radio club. So to answer your question he came in the restaurant the day before he was found dead, and on hearing that is when I called you about his car being in my lot."

"Jimmy will you mind if I stop by in the morning about 8:30 and talk to some of these guys that come in regularly, to see if any of them can help us in our investigation?"

"Absolutely no objection Jack, I will do anything that will help find Horace's killer. He was a personal friend of mine. I am sure they will all be anxious to cooperate. I will hold a booth open for you near where the men almost always sit so you can open a dialog with any of them."

At 8:30 the next morning, Detective Jack Truitt and Agent Bob Spedden arrived at the restaurant and were asked to join the men in the rear of the restaurant at their usual gossip center having their breakfast. They were unaware that a booth had been set aside for Jack. They were just anxious to ask Jack questions about the murders.

Jack introduced agent Bob Spedden of the FBI, to the men. After they had all ordered a breakfast, Bob asked the men if they had noticed anything unusual about Horace when they all last had breakfast with him.

One of the men, Bill Mitchell, a house painting contractor said, "Jack, I saw nothing unusual about him that morning. Horace asked me when my painting crew would finish work on his No.2 broiler house roof that needed to be painted because of rust."

"As we left together for our cars, he was telling me that he would like for it to be done before some the chickens in that house went to Perdue's processing plant that weekend; because there was always a lot of dust when they loaded the broilers."

"Horace walked out of the restaurant with me and we talked for a few minutes about the paint job before I got to my car."

"I don't remember seeing anyone in the area when I got in my car, but when I drove around the building to go to work, I saw Horace standing next to a car parked next to his own car and he was talking with someone in that car."

"I did not recognize the car and could not see who was in the car, except I do remember that he had his arm out the window as if he was handing or pointing out something for Horace to look at."

"I thought nothing of that and I am certain that Horace knew him or had business with him. I can't for the life of me even tell you what make of car it was, or even its' color for that matter. I didn't recognize the man."

Jim Elliott, a local barber said, "Before I left the restaurant, I saw through the window when Horace got in a car with someone and they drove out of the parking lot together."

"Like Bill told you, I can't remember the maker of the car but I am sure it was a clean four door black car and that it had some sort of sticker on the rear bumper. I do know that the license plate was not a Delaware tag, but again, I can't recall what state it was. I think it may have been a Maryland tag, but that is only a guess."

"They were backing out at the time and were gone off together before I left the restaurant. Horace's car was still there when I left. They had not come back to the restaurant while I was there."

Agent Spedden asked, "Can you remember what the sticker on the rear bumper was?"

"No, but I think it was mostly green in color. It could have been just a sport team logo like the Philadelphia Eagles, I really can't remember."

"I do remember that Horace was holding what appeared to be a newspaper as if he was pointing to something on the paper to the guy in the car with him. Maybe it was a story in the paper about the girls that were murdered. Bill said that Horace was outside the car when he left, but Horace was in the car on the passenger side when the two of them drove off. Horace's car was still in the parking lot when they drove off."

"I remember seeing that bumper sticker and I agree that it was green in color. It could have been a sticker for the Philadelphia Eagles, or maybe the Boston Celtics. I really can't say but my bet would be that it was one of the Philadelphia Eagles stickers. I had no reason to look at it closely."

After breakfast, agent Spedden asked, "Jack, do any of the people down here in lower Delaware, follow the Philadelphia Eagles or the Boston Celtics? Is that a common sticker down here?"

"Yes a lot of us do, especially the Philadelphia Eagles or Baltimore Colts, but there are a lot of Celtic fans down here also. You will find one of those three stickers on many cars down here. In fact I have an Eagles sticker on my personal car."

Then loudly, Martin Baker, a local furniture store salesman laughingly interrupted, "Mr. Spedden, I think you better find out where Jack was on the days of the murders and the color of his car."

Jack Wingate, a local barber interrupted the laughing, "Hey wait a minute, I just thought of something. I saw that guy sitting in his car when I went out of the restaurant. I didn't get a clear view of him, but I did notice that he was reading a newspaper."

"What really caught my attention was that he was wearing sun glasses and it was a gloomy day. That is all I can remember, I left before Horace did because I had to go home to take my wife to the dentist for an appointment. Horace was still in here when I left."

No one else in the group had anything to add and the interviews ended. Jack and the agent thanked them all for their cooperation and requested that if they could think or hear anything else about that morning to contact the police chief.

Back at the station, agent Carle mentioned that he was really puzzled, saying that, "At first I thought we had a sex offender as the killer, and we have been busy tracking down all the area's sex offenders on the files."

"In the local area there are only three sex offenders that we are aware of and all three of them are listed as child molesters. But now because Horace was killed, evidently but not proven, by the same person, the question now is why would he kill Horace?"

"Bill, I know that you were a friend of both Horace and his wife Helen in college, but is there a possibility that Horace's wife may have had anything to do with Horace's death. She is certainly the one who would most likely benefit from Horace's death and they were reported as having marital difficulties and in the midst of a divorce battle? It has also been reported that Horace was messing around with both of the women who were murdered."

"Yes Jack that is certainly a possibility, and one that we must follow up on, but, I honestly believe after talking with Helen, that is not the answer. We must also keep in my mind the fact that Mrs. Hastings' family is wealthy in their own right and I can't believe that money played any part in his murder in so far as Mrs. Hastings is concerned. At least I certainly hope that she had nothing to do with his death or the death of the two women."

"We will however, verify that there have been no withdrawals from her accounts of large amounts of cash that could have been given to a hired killer."

"Mr. Carle, isn't there also a possibility that Mrs. Hastings may have had something to do with the killing of the two women? Aren't they both said to have been friendly to Horace and just perhaps Mrs. Hastings was upset about that and wanted them killed?"

"Yes, that is definitely a good motive but if Helen was involved, she would have to have an accomplice. She surely could not have dragged Horace's body down that dirt road where he was found alone or the strength to strangle the women. I am working on just such a person who could have helped her do that; and I will have a report on that after I can make contact with him. But would she want both of the women and Horace killed?"

"It is extremely rare for a rapist to get involved with both men and women, and also remember that the women were strangled by a wire and Horace was shot."

Why would he not have shot the women as well? I am not completely convinced that the murders were all committed by the same person, but their all being classmates certainly points to a single murderer. We will have some of our answers when we get the DNA studies."

"Oh, I almost forgot to mention that the Forensic team stated that it was impossible for Mr. Hastings to have shot himself because he could not have positioned the gun in a position that would have the trajectory they found and oddly enough the Coroner reports he was shot with a 45 caliber and the gun found nearby was a 32 caliber. It now appears he was shot by someone at a very close range standing in back of him, and then there was an attempt to make it look like a suicide."

"That attempt to make it look like a suicide, would also appear to me that Mrs. Hastings was not involved. Why would she want to cut herself out of a large amount of life insurance money which would not be paid if it was a suicide? I read that the policy was well over a million dollars."

Agent Spedden said, "Well if you will remember the scene disproved a suicide, but just perhaps, the killer realized it would be proven not as a suicide and was setup with that in mind just to confuse us."

"Two ladies and then a man in separate murders with different modes of killing puzzle me. We must find out what is prompting these killings. I think we need to go down the list of students and see if we can figure out what is driving this killer. I agree with Bill that there just may possibly be two murderers involved in these cases."

"At any rate, the murderer is surely upset about something and he appears to be taking his motive out on classmates. I will still bet that our suspect is a member of that same class."

Detective Truitt replied. "That is my opinion also. But why would he wait five years to do it? It must be over something that has happened recently. I am now interviewing each member of the class to see if they know of any hatred among their class mates. But then again, perhaps the killer waited the five years because he may not live in Seaford and has a grudge that he still holds after five years."

Agent Carle told Jack and the team which would be doing the interviews, "That's a good approach; but the interviewers must remember when asking questions based on statements of other persons being interviewed; to ask questions in such a way that the killer could not be made aware that we were digging for anything that could be pointed to him, if he was indeed the murderer. Make the person being interviewed think that you suspect it was someone else."

"I fear the murderer may try to kill anyone in the class that would know of his real motive, if the suspect is indeed a classmate, or he feels that we already have something against him."

Jack injected, "I'm a little confused in what you are saying Bill. If for example, we learn through an earlier interview with another student, that the person we are interviewing now was somehow at odds with the earlier person, that we should not mention that accusation for a response even if we don't say names."

"Yes, that is exactly what I mean, Jack. We don't want to put anyone interviewed against another because that may result in another murder by a suspect taking action to eliminate that person if it would possibly incriminate him."

"The question would have to be put to the person being interviewed in such a manner that he or she would not be aware that an accusation against the person being interviewed had been made."

"Ok, I get what you are driving at. Thanks."

"I have a list of all the members of the class, and information as how to contact them. On the list you will note I have scratched off several names. Those scratched off have already been eliminated as a suspect. For example, Fred Dyson has been proven to have been on an air base in Texas. He is in the Air Force and did not attend the reunion. It has been confirmed that he was on the base in Texas."

"We will still interview him later for anything he may remember from his days in school here in Seaford if ut becomes necessary."

"There are four names on the list who for one reason or another, failed to respond to the invitation to the reunion and did not attend the reunion. I feel that perhaps they have a reason for not attending and we should interview these four with the thought that one of them may have a grudge against the class. I have them identified as not at reunion."

"Do give these four individuals a lot of attention and see if you can determine their whereabouts on the dates of the three murders. All others on the list were at the reunion party, and should be interviewed singularly. In fact, I feel that all interviews should be on a one by one basis."

"Let's get started men; we must get this guy quickly because it appears he is mad at the class itself. Lord only knows just what he intends to do next. We also need to find that fellow from Wilmington. Robert Miller, number 24 on your list. He was supposed to attend the reunion but failed to attend even though he was seen in Seaford a few days before the reunion."

"He has been missing now for almost two weeks. I sure hope that he isn't a fourth victim of the class to have been murdered and out there somewhere. I hope I am wrong about that. I will start working on him myself."

"Bill, maybe he was the murderer and took off to get away from it all."

"Yes, I was thinking of that possibility too."

FOUR

THERE WERE NINE names on the list to be interviewed that were members of the class of 1984 and did not live in Seaford or the lower Delaware area. The interviews were conducted at the residences of the individuals by the District branch of the FBI in those states where the person to be interviewed resided.

The classmate living the farthest from Seaford was Fred Dyson who was in the Air Force and stationed in Universal City, Texas at the Randolph AFB. It had already been established that he was in Texas and on the base during the time of all three murders; but they wanted to interview him to see if he could give then a reason or motive for the murders that may have been created back in high school.

Dyson was asked if he had any suggestions as to who could have committed the murders and he replied, "I cannot believe anyone in our class would do such a thing. But the only possible suspect that comes to my mind would be Oliver Hill."

The FBI agent conducting the interview asked, "Why Oliver Hill?"

"Well I am not accusing him of anything, but the kid was always against everything and everybody most of the time. He was a very negative person if that is the right phrase. He kept mostly to himself, he was a sissy, and as far as I know, never dated a girl in high school."

"He was a very tall but skinny boy who, wore dark glasses most of the time and always wore the strangest clothes. Everyone teased him all the time just to get him ranting and raving; perhaps he is holding a grudge over the teasing that he got in school. He got a lot of that."

The agent made a note of Fred's description of Oliver as being tall and skinny, and underlined it with a yellow pen when he had the statement typed up.

"I remember one time he dyed his hair green. What a sight that was. He received so much hazing over that he came to school a few days later with his hair dyed red on one side and blue on the other side."

"I am sure he did that just to get even with us. He really was quite an ugly boy. He had one deformed eye. One was bigger than the other and it sort of stuck out further than the regular size eye. That's why none of the girls wanted anything to do with him."

"How tall would you guess he was?"

"Oh, I would guess about 6 feet 4. I do know that

Horace Hastings, John Bennett, Charles Baker, and we other boys who were into sports, tried our best to get him interested in basketball and football but he wanted nothing to do with sports. He preferred being in the band and he loved music."

"The only time that I ever saw him really get mad was when a few of us boys were at the Seaford Pool Hall and Oliver was playing pool with a stranger for money."

"Oliver was a better pool player than any of us; but we enjoyed watching him beating all the strangers when they came in the pool hall claiming to be pool sharks."

"Oliver would give most of them a lesson real quick. One night he had just beat a stranger quickly for a good size bet, as I recall, and after Oliver won the game, the man told Oliver, 'Well I just learned a good lesson, never play pool with a guy who can look at the cue ball with one eye and the ball he wants to hit with the other one at the same time. Oliver hit the man on the back with his cue stick. Oliver didn't like anyone to kid him about his deformed eye and of course we kids did not do that."

"Was he ever involved in any fights over the hazing that you mentioned earlier, or about his deformity? OR he got?"

"Oh heavens no, he was really a pussycat even though he was big for his age. He did all his arguing with words. He could cuss like a drunken sailor. Some of the boys thought he was queer but I never heard anything to prove that. Like I said before about hitting that man in the pool hall with his cue stick; that was the only time I ever saw him really get physical."

"You mentioned that he took a lot of hazing in high school. Was there any particular person that hazed him often?"

"Not that I can recall. He pretty much stayed to himself. The only friend that I can remember he had in school was a boy named Harry Black. Harry was in the band with Oliver and they often played in band jobs at local events. They were both really good musicians."

"I always suspected that the two of them were messing with drugs but to the best of my knowledge they were never caught doing them."

"I really don't think Oliver was gay, I think he was just a screwball. I bet he didn't attend the reunion. He was just not interested in any class projects. Did he go?"

"I don't know for sure." The agent replied, knowing full well that Oliver was on the listed of those not attending the reunion. His FBI training had instructed him never to reveal any information to persons being interviewed that was not common knowledge.

An interview that same afternoon with Toby Foster revealed that Toby had attended the reunion with Jeanne Records, but Jeanne had been taken home following the reunion and her parents said that Jeanne did not become missing until Saturday night, She left home Saturday afternoon to go shopping at the mall and failed to come home. They had not seen her since. Her date at the reunion, Toby Foster was playing golf at the country club in a foursome and was playing cards with the same group of men on Saturday night.

When asked about Jeanne dancing so much with Horace at the reunion; Toby said that did not bother him at all, because he didn't like to dance. He said that he and Jeanne went out a lot together but they had never discussed any intention of getting engaged or married. He said he thought he was not ready for that. He said he liked the bachelor life but had made up his mind to give her an engagement ring on her birthday.

He said that was what he liked about Jeanne she appeared to like the free life style as he did, adding that she was very upset about Harriet's death.

When Toby was asked if Jeanne had mentioned any thoughts on why Harriet was murdered, he told the agents that she thought it may have had something to do over a pregnancy. Harriet had told Jeanne that she thought she was pregnant but refused to tell Jeanne who the father. She told Jeanne that she would be marrying the father soon.

The other members of the class not attending the reunion were now living in Laurel, Delaware, Berlin, Maryland, Assateague, Virginia, Lebanon, Tennessee, Richmond Virginia, Columbia, South Carolina, Durham, North Carolina, Ogden, Utah, and Tampa, Florida.

The classmate that lived in Laurel, Nickolas Parham was interviewed first because of the fact that Harriet's car was found in Laurel. Nick said that he did not attend the reunion because he had already planned to take his family on vacation that same week. They were on a camping trip along the Skyline Drive, in Virginia and camped in the Great Smokey National Park for over a week.

The others who did not attend the reunion were all interviewed with the exception of Harry Black who could not be located at his place of residence in Tampa Florida, and Bob Miller who was still missing. Those persons that were interviewed were all confirmed as being at home during the time of the reunion or were elsewhere at the time of the reunion and all were cleared with positive evidence of not being in Seaford at the time of the murders.

They had no suggestions to offer as a motive for the murders and most stated that it was too costly for them to attend the reunion back in Delaware.

Harry Black was not at his home address in Tampa Florida. It was unknown where he was. The Tampa police reported that Harry was a known drug addict and had been arrested several times for drug trafficking.

Harry's friends told the agent that he was thought to be in California but they did not know where. The agent was well aware that they would not have told him where Harry was even if they did know.

The Tampa police told the FBI agent that all of Harry's friends were addicts and stated that they would watch for him at his Tampa hangouts and would pick him up for questioning if and when the agents should locate Harry later.

The police said, to their knowledge, Harry did not

have an automobile and they felt certain that they would have Harry for them soon because they had an addict that would always help the police for a few dollars under the table to buy his own drugs. They had paid him for information many times, and his information was always reliable.

The first five interviews in the Seaford area were with those local members that also did not attend the reunion. The five were John Bennett, Franklin Morris, Harlan Griffin, Douglas Weaver, and Ethel Williams Givens. They were instructed to see if any of them had a grudge against the class or any of its members and that was why they did not attend the reunion.

Agent Bill Carle, set up a time to interview John Bennett on the list and arrived at John's home at the agreed time. John was waiting for him and answered the door.

"John, I am certain that you have heard or read of the murder of three of your classmates over the past few weeks."

"Yes, I have both heard and read about it, they were all classmates of mine. I hope that you get the guy that did it real soon. My wife is terrified."

First John, "Allow me to introduce myself I am William Carle, an agent of the Federal Bureau of Investigation. I have been assigned to these three local murder cases and I would like to ask you a few questions that may help us in our investigation.

Please know that we plan to interview everyone in the

class, and you have not been singled out for questioning. Also by law, I must advise you of your rights and I want you to know that we are seeking information only.

Carle read him his rights and proceeded with the interview after John had acknowledged orally that he had been given his rights.

"Thank you John, the reason that we are questioning everyone in this class is because all three of the murders were committed around the time of a class reunion and we think that there must be a connection to your class."

"We have been told that you did not attend the reunion. Is there a reason that you did not attend."

"That's easy Mr. Carle, my wife Elizabeth, is expecting a baby any day now, and she was not comfortable in going to a party so near term. By the way, she is also a member of the class."

"That seems like a good reason to me, and yes, I knew that she was a member of the class, but my instructions require that all members of the class must be interviewed separately and she would have been interviewed in a day or so; but if she is so near term, perhaps, I can interview her today after your interview. Is she available to talk with me with such short notice after we finish here?"

"Yes, she is upstairs I will go tell her; if that is all right, so she can prepare for it, if that is Ok."

"Sure thing,"

When John returned downstairs, he told the agent, "Yes she will be ready, she just needs to put on some presentable clothes she was in her house robe."

"Great, let's get started again. John, do you have any thoughts about these murders. Can you think of any reason why someone would want to kill them?"

"Not that I can think of offhand. I was told that the two girls were both raped and when I was told that, I just assumed we had a rapist in the area. Both of those women were certainly attractive and single. They enjoyed parties, or at least they did in high school, I really don't know much about their activities now."

"I seldom see them these days. It is a mystery to me why Horace was murdered, especially after reading in the paper that he was not robbed. Horace always had money with him as he is a very prosperous farmer."

"Do you know of any connection between Horace and the two women?"

"Not that I know about. Horace was always a ladies' man in high school and he dated most all of them. He was a star football player and all the girls were attracted to him. I do know that in high school, Horace would have been considered a very close friend of both Harriet and Jeanne. I remember he dated both of them at times."

"He married a classmate as I did. He went to the University of Delaware and in his junior or senior year at Delaware, he married a girl named Helen Groton. Helen was a very pretty girl and I think she was one of his best friends while in school.

"Yes, that is true John, I attended the University of Delaware too and I knew and dated Helen Groton myself while I was at Delaware in her freshman year and part of her sophomore year. My parents moved from Wilmington, Delaware during my sophomore year and I took my credits and transferred to the University of Tennessee to be close to my family. I lived off campus with them to save money."

"We exchanged several letters after I transferred to Tennessee and she told me that she was seeing Horace and I later heard that they were married. I really didn't know Horace real well, but I knew of him through Helen."

"But let's get back to the reason why I am here, can you think of anything that could explain why he or either of the women was murdered?"

"That's quite a coincidence; in your being assigned to a case investigating old college friends isn't it?"

"Well not actually, I read the brief on the case and when I recognized their names, I requested the assignment. What can you tell me about Horace? Do you have any idea as to why someone would want to see him killed?"

"A lot of the boys would have liked to have killed Horace in high school because all of us had to play second fiddle after him with the girls. Just kidding of course, he really was a swell guy and a great football player. I can't imagine why someone wanted to kill him."

"Can you recall any particular boys in the class that ever got in a fight or had a strong argument with Horace over a girl?"

"Oh no, we were all jealous of Horace but we all admired him and we, or me for certain, considered him a very close friend. Horace was the kind of boy that would do anything for you. He always contributes generously to local worthy projects. He is also the largest donor in our church. We attend the same church, although he does not attend regularly anymore because he and his wife are separated, but he is still at all of the church business meetings."

"John, I guess you know that one of the questions I have to ask, is, where were you on the dates of the murders?"

"Yes, I guessed that you would be asking that question and I have been trying to remember exactly and as far as I can recall, in the daylight hours I would have been at work on the home of George Collins, where I was doing some plumbing work, I have a plumbing business you probably know."

"Yes, I am aware of that."

"I would have been at the Collins home, when both Harriet and Jeanne were killed and was also doing plumbing on the days around the date of Horace's murder. I will have to check my records if you need exactly which houses I was doing plumbing at; but one place that I do recall, was at Dr. Jack Owens' office. I know I was there for several days. Then in the evening hours over the last month, I was always at home with my wife. I can't be out now with her condition as it is."

"Tell me John, when you were in school was you aware of any of the boys that were - how shall I ask it, overly sexed or who may have had a reputation of being too aggressive with girls?"

"You mean anyone who could have raped the two women; no, not that I can think of or have heard about; except my wife did tell me that Homer Price, a boy in her class, tried to rape her when they were on a date once, but she fought him off. She never dated him again."

"Is Homer Price still living in the area, and is he married?"

"Yes, he lives on Stein highway near the Baptist Church. He married a girl from Bridgeville, Delaware. I don't know her name. He is a member of our class too."

"One last question John; if you knew him what can you tell me about Robert Miller?"

"I knew him well in my school days. I don't know where he lives today. Robert was all business he was a bookworm, a top student in our class. He never played any school sports. I think he was a golfer, but I never played any golf with him that I can recall."

"He dated a girl named Kathy Black all through high school. They were real lovebirds. I don't remember either of them ever dating anyone else. We were certain that they would be the first in the class to get married; but some time in her senior year Kathy left Seaford, and went down south somewhere to live."

"We never knew for sure why she left; but the local gossip at the time was that she had been raped. Later we found out that was not true. At least she denied being raped and later run off with a boy from down South and got married. Hey I forgot about that until just now. Maybe that is a connection for you"

"At any rate, she did not graduate with us. She has now moved back to Seaford and works at the library. She is the information clerk on the front desk, Kathy was married after she left Seaford, but her marriage ended in a divorce. She has a child, a boy I think, from that marriage. Perhaps she may be able to help you."

"I have not seen or heard of her dating any one since she returned. Poor Robert was really depressed when she left. He quit going to all school events after that. When he graduated he moved away. I haven't seen him since school days."

"John I think I have all I need and I wonder if your wife is ready. Remember that I have to interview her privately."

"Yes, I remember. I will see if she is ready. I'll go get her and then leave."

"Great John and I do appreciate your information and please remember you can contact me at any time if you have anything to add that may be of help to us."

Returning with his wife, "Mr. Carle, this is my wife Elizabeth, we call her Betty. Betty this is Mr. William Carle of the FBI. He wants to talk to you about our class mates at high school and the murders of Jeanne, Harriett, and Horace. When he was in college he knew both Horace and Horace's wife Helen. I will be out in the shop when you are finished so just ring the bell when you are done or you need me."

"First Mrs. Bennett, allow me to properly introduce myself for the tape. I am William Carle, an agent of the

Federal Bureau of Investigation. I have been assigned to the three local murder cases and I would like to ask you a few questions that may help us in our investigation."

"Please know that we plan to interview everyone in the class and you have not been singled out for questioning. Also by law I must advise you of your rights."

William read her the rights and proceeded with the interview after Elizabeth had acknowledged orally that she had been given her rights.

"Thank you Mrs. Bennett, the reason that we are questioning everyone in your high school class is because all three of the murders were committed around the time of your class reunion and we think that there must be a connection to your class."

"We have been told that you did not attend the reunion. Is there a reason that you did not attend other than your being so near term?"

"No, Mr. Carle that is the only reason. I would have gone had I not been so near term as you said."

"I am sure that you and John have both read about the murders of three of your classmates. Can you tell me if you have any ideas as to who would have done such a thing?"

"Well when I heard about the first two, I thought of a boy in our class named Homer Price because the newspaper reported that both of the girls had been raped. I thought that he was the only boy in our class that would have done such a thing."

"Why would you think it might be Homer Price Mrs. Bennett?"

"Please call me Betty I will be more at ease if you do that. When we were all in high school I once went on a date with Homer, to the movies, and on the way home he drove me to a wooded area which we kids referred to as "lovers lane" on what we call "The Island", just east of Seaford. In fact the newspaper said that is near where Harriet was found. That is why I thought of Homer."

"We kissed a few times; but Homer wanted to go further than that and of course I refused him. I was a virgin and not that kind of girl. He fought me and even ripped some of my clothing. I was able to get away from him and I ordered him to take me home, or I would tell the police that he tried to rape me."

"I think he was about to rape me if I had not hit him so hard. I actually cut his upper lip and he was bleeding badly, but he took me home without saying another word."

"Mr. Carle I do hope if what I am about to tell you is not of help to you, that it will not be made public unless it will help you find your killer. What I am about to tell you has been a secret that I have kept every since it happened in high school."

"I understand Betty, and I will do as you say unless it is necessary to solve these murders."

"Thank you Mr. Carle. Here goes. A few days after my experience with Homer, I was telling a friend of mine named Kathy Black about the incident and Kathy confessed to me that Homer had indeed raped her after she too had refused his advances."

"He had volunteered to take her home from a basketball game when her regular beau Robert Miller was sick in bed with a cold."

"Yes Mr. Carle I thought that Homer may have been the one, but after Horace was reported killed, I decided that it must not have been Homer. Homer would have no reason to kill Horace. Please don't tell my husband, John about what I just said."

"John knows about what Homer did to you."

"Yes, but he does not know what Homer did to Kathy Black. No one, to my knowledge, but I know about that. Kathy was my very closest friend and confided to me about that rape. She asked me never to tell anyone because she didn't want Robert Miller who was her boyfriend to hear about it for fear that Robert would have confronted Homer."

"I never told anyone even John, about that even when it was rumored she had been raped and that was why she moved away years back then."

"Neither Kathy nor I could ever determine how that gossip got started. But anyway, Kathy let everyone believe, that she had eloped with a boy from Virginia and came back to Seaford only after she obtained a divorce. I helped her do that too. I hope that she will not find out that I told you her real story."

"Have no fear Betty I will not tell John or Kathy about that. Do you have any other reason to suspect Homer? Or do you have any reason to suspect anyone else? Can you think of any reason why someone would want to kill those three people?"

"I can't imagine why anyone would want to do such a thing, and if it was one of our classmates who did this; why would he wait five years to rape and kill two girls who lived in Seaford all these years."

"I also find it hard to believe that anyone would hold a grudge or whatever the reason for so long a time."

"That's a question that we too are wondering."

"Betty what more can you tell me about Kathy Black and Robert Miller?"

"Well like I just said, Kathy Black was and still is my closest and dearest friend in Seaford. Kathy and Robert were sweethearts all through high school."

"I can't recall either of them dating anyone else. As I have already mentioned to you, she told me that Homer Price asked to drive her home after a ball game one night because Robert was ill at the time, and that is when she was raped."

"She would not bring charges against Homer because of the embarrassment. She quit dating Robert and after about a month when she discovered she was pregnant she moved to Virginia. She and I kept in contact and she told me the whole story and asked me not to mention that to anyone and she begged me not to tell Robert or anyone else."

"I am sure that Kathy and Robert would have married if this had not happened. I was always hoping that she and

Robert could have gotten back together, but Robert left Seaford brokenhearted when he graduated. Please don't let her know I told you this, I mention it only because Homer may be your killer, at least of the women. I don't know why he would have killed Horace."

"Betty your comments will never be mentioned to Kathy or others. Betty, if you think of anything else that might help us in finding this killer, please call me at any time."

"Here's a card with numbers where I can be reached at any time. I hope all goes well with you and the coming baby. And Betty; don't tell anyone what you have told me."

"Don't worry, I won't do that."

Agent Robert Spedden had interviewed four of the names on his list and all four could offer no information to help the investigators. All four also could not offer any suggestions as to why the three victims would have been murdered.

Their whereabouts during the period of the murders had been received and was being confirmed by other agents.

FIVE

Agent Spedden was now interviewing Mary Smoot. Mary was a teller at a local bank and was still unmarried but was dating a man from Delmar, Maryland. Mary attended the reunion. She went alone.

"Mary I want to properly introduce myself. I am Robert Spedden, an agent of the Federal Bureau of Investigation. I have been assigned to work on the three local murder cases and I would like to ask you a few questions that may help us in our investigation."

"Please know that we plan to interview everyone in the class and you have not been singled out; for questioning. We are questioning everyone in the class. Also by law I must advise you of your rights."

Robert read her the rights and proceeded with the interview after Mary had acknowledged orally that she had been given her rights.

"Mary we are concerned that these murders may possibly have been committed by the same individual and that individual, for some reason is upset with some of your high school classmates."

"I am questioning you to see if you can possibly give us an insight as to why these classmates of yours were killed. Can you think of any reason why they may have been killed?"

"Mr. Spedden I was going to call the police about an incident that happened just a few weeks ago, but to be honest, I was afraid to do so, because I was afraid to get involved."

"Have no fear Mary, nothing that you tell us will get to anyone outside our office, you can speak freely. We will then follow up on any information you give us and determine if it will assist our efforts to solve these murders. Please tell me what is on your mind."

"Ok, A few weeks ago, I was on a date with a friend, Mark Haley, and we stopped in the Flagship Restaurant after seeing a movie at the Layton Theater to have a nightcap. When we parked and were about to enter the restaurant, we witnessed a fight in the parking lot."

"It was a fight between Horace Hastings and Douglas Weaver. Both were in our class. Horace easily beat Douglas and Douglas yelled out to Horace "I'll get you, you SOB", or something threatening close to that. He was cursing like a drunken sailor as he drove off in his car."

"My date Mark and I went over to Horace after

Douglas drove off and asked Horace if he was Ok and asked what all of that was about."

"Horace told us that when he arrived at the restaurant to pick up a takeout order, Douglas and Harriet O'Brien were just leaving the restaurant and that they were arguing loudly about something and all of a sudden Douglas started pushing and hitting Harriet. That is when Horace said he ran over and started to restrain Douglas and the fight started."

"Harriet thanked Horace, and sped off in her car after the fight, so we never did know what the argument was over. Apparently Harriet and Douglas had their own cars there so it must have started inside the restaurant. Harriet did not appear to have been hurt but Douglas had torn her blouse in the scuffle. Horace had a scratch on his cheek that bled just a little but was not hurt otherwise. I don't know if Douglas was hurt or not. But Horace did knock him to the ground and that was the end of the fight."

"Well thank you for that information. I see on my list that Douglas failed to attend the reunion. Now Mary think very carefully; have you told anyone about that fight?"

"No not a soul. The next day I heard of Harriet's death, and I was scared to death that Douglas had done it and wondered if he had seen Mark or me. I was afraid that he would try to get me to shut me up. I have really been scared to death every since I heard that both Harriet and Horace had been killed."

"Let's get back to your date. Do you think that he has mentioned the fight or any of the events to anyone?"

"I am sure that he has not. Mark is from Chicago and he flew out of Philadelphia airport the next morning before the news of Harriet came out and I have not talked with him since. I last saw him the night of the fight. I doubt if he even knew about the murders."

"You said that Mark was your date that evening, what is your relationship with him?"

"Mark is just a very good friend of mine, I met him at college and we have been in touch every since those days. Mark is married and has two children. His wife was my roommate at the University of Maryland. That is how I met him."

"His wife and I still communicate and visit every once in awhile. Mark was in Salisbury, Maryland on business, he installs hospital medical equipment of some sort in hospitals and his wife called me to tell me that he would be near me. I told her to have him call me, and we could have dinner together. He did call me to see if I could have dinner with him that night, because he had to be back in Chicago the next day."

"Mary I hope that you will not reveal this story to anyone. I am sure that you now know why. It may endanger anyone you tell and, may endanger you as well. I will ask Chief Daley to place your house under surveillance until further notice, just in case Douglas saw you in the parking lot. So if you see a strange car or van parked near your house or following you to and from work, please don't be concerned."

"When you are being followed the vehicle immediately in back of you may be our man. If it is our man he will turn his lights on and then off to let you know all is okay."

"Is that understood Mary? We will make sure that no harm comes to you, but the most important thing you can do is to not mention any of this to anyone. Again, are you sure you have not told anyone any portion of it?"

"Yes, I am positive I have not told anyone. I was too scared, believe me."

When agent Spedden returned to the station, he asked for an immediate surveillance to be started on Mary Smoot's apartment and that she should be followed to and from her place of employment, and her residence as well.

He was not about to let Mary out of their sight. Immediately after he had that setup he, detective Short, and agent Carle left for the firm where Douglas worked with a warrant for his arrest.

They were prepared to arrest him on the spot as a suspect in the murder of Horace Hastings; but his employer, a vehicle parts company named Mason's Auto Parts, told them Douglas was not at work and that he was on vacation. He started vacation just the day before and he was not due back to work until July 9th.

The store manager said, "Yes, he and the others all left together on Saturday morning to attend the NASCAR races in Daytona Beach Florida, so that they would be at the track for race week. They are in our company car. They should be in Daytona Beach by tonight."

Agent Carle noted that Douglas left after the deaths of Harriet, Jeanne, as well as Horace.

"Do you know where they will be staying in Daytona Beach?"

"Oh yes, the company foots the bill for their tickets and all expenses as an incentive award for their work over the past years. Give me a minute or so and I will get you the motel where they are staying."

He returned with a folder from the motel and gave it to Agent Carle. "They will be at this motel through July 7.

After discussing the situation with the state Attorney General, it was decided that they need not keep Mary under 24 hour surveillance at this time, but they would keep her on a general surveillance.

The Attorney General told them it was apparent that Douglas was not on the run, so they decided to wait and pick Douglas up as soon as he returned to Seaford on the 8th or 9th of July because their suspicion was entirely based on one person's statement.

In the meantime, they would have the Florida branch office verify that he was in Florida at the motel with the other Mason Auto Parts employees. They were given the name and address of the motel where they would be staying.

Agent Carle completed seven more interviews and

all seven were with those attending the reunion. None of the seven could offer any explanation or suggestions that may have assisted the investigation. All seven were able to provide where they were during the entire week of the murders. The statements of the seven were being checked.

Three of the women interviewed stated that they were sure that no one in their class could have done the murders of the women and they were sure it had to be a sex predator.

When asked about Horace's death; two of them stated he must have been killed over his wealth, but when told that he was not robbed and had a large sum of money on him, they could think of no other reason, but one man stated it may have been over the separation of Horace and his wife.

The Florida FBI office reported that the men they inquired about were in Florida and staying at the motel that they were asked to verify. No further action was taken but they would maintain a watch on their activities and advise when they checked out of the motel. They were prepared to arrest Douglas at any time if requested.

The next day agent Carle's his first interview was with Martha Phillips. Martha worked at a store in the Seaford Shopping Center Mall. She was divorced from her first husband and was living with George Thompson, an apprentice electrician, for a local contractor.

During the interview Martha stated, "My friend

in high school, Sally Truitt had become pregnant by a Georgetown, Delaware boy named Alfred Warrington.

Alfred was the son of a very wealthy lawyer who lived and practiced law in the Sussex County seat of Georgetown."

"His family offered to pay for an abortion for Sally but she refused to have the abortion; instead she hired a lawyer to sue the Warrington's for child support and their promise of a college education for her unborn child."

"The Warrington's offered to pay a large onetime payment that they deemed sufficient to provide for the child and provide funds for a four year University of Delaware enrollment if she would drop the law suit."

Martha told agent Carle, "Rumor at the time had it at $150,000. I really don't know the total amount, anyway, Sally accepted the offer, whatever amount it was, and dropped out of school to care for the baby who was born in her senior year. The same year the rest of her classmates graduated. Sally did not graduate with her class. She is now married."

"I am telling you this because I was told about it by Jeanne Records herself. Jeanne was my best friend at the time. And because Jeanne was one of the murder victims perhaps Harriet was also pregnant by that same Georgetown man, Alfred Warrington because I do know for a fact that Harriet had been dating Alfred at times. Maybe he didn't want his parents to know that he had done it again."

Agent Carle asked, "When were you told this Martha?"

"Jeanne told me on the day that Harriet's body was found. We were talking about Harriet and she said that Harriet told her she was pregnant but she did not say by whom and Jeanne and I were wondering if it was Alfred and if he had anything to do with her death."

Agent Carle made a note that Martha had talked with Jeanne on the day after Harriet's body was found and that would have been the day of the reunion.

"Did anyone else hear about that story?"

"Not from me, I have no idea if Jeanne told anyone else about that or not. She was one of the girls that was murdered you know. In fact she was murdered the day after we had lunch together. I have really been scared to death every since I learned of her death."

"I would advise you and hope you will keep that information a secret until all of this is resolved."

"I sure will, I don't want anyone to know that I know anything."

On agent Carle's return to the station, he and agent Spedden decided to travel over to Georgetown to interview Alfred Warrington. They also decided not to question him about the prior paternity story that Martha had given to agent Carle, but would limit the interview at this time to questions regarding his dating Harriet and to go from there.

As they prepared to leave Chief Daley asked agent

Carle if he could step in his office for a minute, and Bill went in and Chief Daley closed the door.

"Bill, I just got some information from a source in the bank, that on June 16, Mrs. Helen Hastings, Horace's wife, withdrew fifteen hundred dollars from her personal savings account."

"In view of your reported relationship with Helen, I wanted you to be the first to know that, and I want you to check up on it."

"I have no reason at the moment to put that before the team, so I have not told anyone about it because the poor girl has enough on her shoulders already without adding to her load."

"I trust you will get the answer just why she did that. There has to be a reason. I have been told that she has never made a withdrawal from her savings in the past."

"Oh dear God, I do hope she has a reason for having done that. I remember Bob asking me of the possibility that she may have hired someone to kill the women. Chief I will have an answer for you in the next few days. I thank you for letting me get the answer. If word got out on that I am afraid that some of our team would want to make her a suspect without investigation."

"Yes, and that is exactly why I gave it to you. I am confident that she is not a suspect."

"Chief, I am on my way to Georgetown this afternoon for an interview with Alfred Warrington, and will get on that as soon as we get back. Thanks for letting me get you the answer. Helen does have so much on her shoulders.

I am certain I will have you an answer, I think I can get the answer without her knowing that we are questioning the withdrawal."

When the agents Carle and Spedden arrived in Georgetown about thirty minutes later, they went to Alfred's residence which they learned was just three blocks from his parent's home. He had an apartment in one of his grandfather's rental buildings.

He was not at home so they then went to his parent's home and were told that he had gone to Rehoboth Beach to make some repairs on a home there that his father owned and rented.

They got the address from Alfred's mother and then drove east to the beach, located the home, and found Alfred working inside the house. They were certain that his mother had called him they were coming.

They introduced themselves as FBI Agents and told Alfred they were investigating the death of Harriet O'Brien, because according to reports they had obtained, he was dating Harriet at the time of her death.

"According to the information we have obtained on Miss O'Brien, we understand that you were dating Miss O'Brien at the time of her death. Is that true?"

"Not exactly, I have dated Harriet many times but I have not dated her since March of this year. She was also dating someone else over there in Seaford at the same time I was dating her and when I called her one day in March for a date she told me that she was seeing someone else. She did not accept my offer to take her out to dinner. I never called her again. I read in the paper that she was dead. Is that why you are questioning me?"

"Yes, but we were told that you were seen with her sometime the week she was killed."

"That's a lie! I haven't seen her since last March, like I said."

The agents had no reports of Alfred being with Harriet near the time of her death but wanted to hear what Alfred's reaction would be.

"Well you know how these reports pop up when something happens like this. We take a lot of them with a grain of salt, so to speak. What can you tell us about Horace Hastings? Horace was the man that was murdered after the women were found murdered."

"I didn't know Horace personally I knew him only through Harriet and the fact that he was a star football player. I played against him in high school football games."

"Tell us Alfred of anything that you think may help us find the murderer. The Coroner told us that Jeanne had been sexually attacked before she was strangled to death. What kind of a girl was she? We know she was single but we would like to know about her habits. Was she the type that dated many men? Are you aware of any relationships that she has had in the last six months or so?"

"Well Harriet was a very pretty girl, and was very active in sports. That is how I met her. I met her at a high school football game a few years back when a group of us went to a fast food restaurant in Seaford after the Seaford and Georgetown high school football game. I think the name was The Spot Diner."

"We had something to eat and I asked her about going out with me. She agreed and that was it. I asked some of the guys that I knew about her and they told me that she was a nice girl, but dated many men. Several of them told me they had sex with her but I am certain they did not."

"Why do you know she didn't?"

"Well when I dated her she stopped me on several dates from trying. In fact I have never had sex with her. She was fun to be with and enjoyed sports as I do. That is why I was attracted to her."

"Well we will know who did have sex with her when we get our DNA tests back. What about the fact that someone mentioned that you were seen with her recently, you said you hadn't seen her since March."

"That's a lie too. We broke it off in March."

"Well Alfred, we must do our job and of course you realize that one of the things we must do is establish where you were over the week of those murders. Can you do that for us now?"

"I sure can. I was nowhere near Seaford on the date of Harriet's murder. I was with my dad in Dover Delaware. He was attending a Democrat Party meeting of some sort and he asked me to go with him because he doesn't like to ride alone or drive at night."

"How do you know the date or if it was the night that Harriet was murdered?"

"I read of it in the newspaper. I was with my dad that

night and most of the next day. I didn't attend the meeting but went to a bar and watched a rerun of a professional football game they were playing on the TV."

"What game was that?"

"I can't remember just now, I watch them all the time."

"Where were you the night that the other woman Jeanne Records was strangled?"

"Strangled, I thought she drowned? I read about her in the newspaper. I didn't know her and I don't think I have ever met her. I didn't know Horace Hastings very well either. Why do you question my whereabouts on the date of their deaths?"

"Simply because they were both Harriet's best friends and the fact that Jeanne was almost always seen with Harriet and according to our information, they were rarely seen apart. We were hoping that you could give us some information about her last several days. We wonder if she knew why Harriet was murdered."

"No, I can't help you with those things. I did not know her, and as I told you I had not seen Harriet since March when we broke up. I had heard that Horace Hastings was always a ladies' man and I would bet he had something to do with her murder. He was married and has children. Perhaps he raped Harriet and then committed suicide. Check with his wife. I heard he was running out on her."

"Why would you say that Alfred, you just told us you hardly knew him and only through Harriet?"

"That's right, I only knew him through Harriet. She was always talking about him. She was always telling me how great a football player he was and how much money he was worth. Things like that."

"Oh, I see. Then you think that he may have been messing around with Harriet and his wife may have found out."

"I didn't say he did, but I would not be surprised."

"Well Bob, do you have any questions for Alfred before we go back to Seaford and check if that DNA test is back yet?."

"Yes, I have a couple of questions. Alfred I realize you just told us that you hardly knew Horace but tell me the truth just how well did you really know Horace Hastings? Did you know him well enough to suspect him as the guy who took Harriet away from you? Maybe she was after Horace's money."

"I told you, I didn't know him personally but Harriet mentioned him on many occasions. I will say that I thought that she had something going on with him. Perhaps he was the one that she was dating. But I was not crazy enough to kill anyone over her."

"Why do you say that they may have had something going? Have you heard anything about Harriet and Horace?"

"Not really, the only reason I said that was that she was always talking about him, how great a football player he was. You know, Horace this, Horace that. I bet if anyone was screwing her it would have been Horace."

"But you said she did not do that sort of thing."

"Well if she did I bet Horace would be the one she did it with. Wilson Rogers, a friend of mine in Georgetown has a boat, really its' a yacht, that he keeps at Indian River where Horace keeps his boat. He told me that Horace has overnight visitors quite often on his yacht and he told me that on one occasion, Horace invited him and his wife over to his boat for drinks."

"He said that Horace introduced both Harriet and Jeanne to him and a man named Greg or something like that. He said that he joined them the next morning to go fishing out of the inlet, and the two women stayed on Wilson's boat while the men fished."

"Did you say that Mr. Rogers lives in Georgetown?"

"Yes, he owns an oil distributorship. His office is on the circle."

"What's the circle?"

"It's actually in the middle of town where four roads intersect and the roads all circle around the square. The courthouse is on the square."

"We will check all of that out, thanks for the information Alfred. Please take this card and if you come up with anything that you think might help us get to the bottom of these murders be sure to call us. By the way what is the make and color of your car?"

"That's it parked right out front – a red Honda 2 door."

"OK, thanks Alfred, we may be back, if other things

come to our attention where you may possibly help. Bill I sure wish we had time for a dip in the Ocean."

On the way back to Seaford Bill asked Bob why he asked about the color of his car.

Bob replied, "For no reason at all. I just wanted to let him think that we knew something about his car just like when you told me about getting back the DNA test results. I knew you were just letting him know that he might be in a fix if he really had sex with Harriet."

"Later we will have to talk to his father about that trip to a political meeting in Dover. By the way his car is not black, so it must not have been his car in which that man was seen talking to Harriet."

'Yes, good thinking; don't forget to add that to the record. I thought that was why you asked him about the color."

"No, just being a good agent. I will add it to the transcript though and I will also add that he tried to cast doubt on Horace as a possible suspect. I had a feeling he was lying. He was being too positive with his answers. It appeared to me that he was scared that we knew something about him. Did you get that impression?"

"Yes, I did and I agree that he was scared and doing his best to put himself away from Harriet and Horace. I made a note that he repeated March several times. Why was he pushing that date? He was well prepared for our arrival for sure. By a call from his mother I would guess."

"Why don't we stop in Georgetown and see if we can talk with the Rogers guy?'

They were lucky Mr. Rogers was in his office and confirmed what Alfred had told them. He told the agents that when he saw the item in the paper, he asked his wife, if that was the same two girls and she said that was who they were. He said that evening on the boat was over a month ago, and he didn't think that had anything to do with their being murdered and raped. He agreed with Alfred in that Horace was a party man and often had overnight guests on the boat."

"Bob I won't be able to have dinner with you this evening, I need to see Helen about something."

"Yeah, I bet you do, you want to eat with her instead of me. You'll do anything for a free meal. But, that's Ok, I'll just stop at the Flagship, maybe I can find a nice pretty gal to join me."

SIX

Agent Carle arrived at Helen's house and she had a dinner on the table waiting for him. She had told him that she would prefer eating at home rather than go out to eat.

During dinner Bill switched their talk from reminiscence to a question on Larry Adams, the man that was helping Helen with her divorce.

"Helen, does Larry have any training in divorce proceedings? Does he have a degree in law?"

"No. He was recommended to me because he had won custody of his children when he and his wife divorced and I was told that any man that can win total custody of children in a divorce had to be pretty knowledgeable."

"Were you paying him to help you?"

"No, he volunteered to help me and refused to take any money when I offered to pay him. He said, I'm no lawyer I just hate to see the divorce lawyers cheat people out of what is rightfully theirs. Like in my case he said that it was my parent's money that made Horace rich."

"Then you never had to pay him any money is that correct?"

"Oh Bill, you are talking like FBI again. No, I never paid him any money. The only money that I ever gave him was $1500.00 to reimburse him for a private investigator he hired to get proof that Horace was committing adultery and some property title work. Larry said we would need that to prove it and with proof we would win full custody."

"Yes, I guess your right Helen. I have been told many times to quit questioning everything someone tells me, but I was really wondering about Larry. I guess I'm just suspicious of anybody that offers free service or something for nothing."

"I will be out of town tomorrow so how about having dinner with me on Thursday night? There's a new Italian restaurant in Dover that several of our team members claim it to be one of the best around. Want to give it a try?"

"Yes Bill that would be worth checking out. I just may play bridge with the ladies tomorrow night. They have been hinting to me that I should start playing again. None of us have played since Horace died. I will make arrangements for a baby sitter for Thursday."

"Great, I will call you about the time, but plan for it

around five thirty. I have to run now I have an interview set up in about an hour."

Back at the police station the next morning, Chief Daley called a meeting to discuss what had been done over the past week, and asked for the results of the interviews.

Agent Carle told the chief what he had found out about Helen's money that was withdrawn from her savings account and they both decided that they would have to determine if he did pay a private investigator or what he did with that money.

The chief told Bill, "You know that may have been used for a private investigator; but it could very well have been as payment for a hit on Horace."

"Yes, I am aware of that but I will be going to Salisbury tomorrow and I will get us answer. Please give me another day or two clear this all up."

"No problem and I do hope you find all to be Ok. We better get in to the meeting I called for."

Chief Daley told the members of the team that a summary of all the interviews to date had been prepared for them and that he felt they may have clues in them that were overlooked. He told them he wanted every member of the team to review all of them again for discrepancies that would require further investigation.

After all the interviews were discussed, the listing and copies of the interviews was prepared and distributed to all of the team members.

First on the list was the interview with John and Betty

Bennett and the chief advised the team, "John told us that he and his wife, both members of the class of 1984, did not attend the reunion because his wife was pregnant and she was very near term."

"John could not give us any information as to who could have raped and killed his three classmates. He told us that he just assumed that a rapist had been involved and that it could have been anyone."

"John went on to say he was puzzled after Horace was murdered because that changed his mind away from his first thought that the murderer was a rapist."

"When we finished talking to John we interviewed his wife, Elizabeth or Betty as she prefers to be called, privately of course, and she expanded on the fact that she thought it was by a rapist but she told us a story that she had not even told her husband."

"She said that when she read in the newspaper that Harriet had been raped, she was reminded that when she was a junior in the high school, she was dating a boy, also in the class, named Homer Price and that he had attempted to rape her but she broke away from him and he drove her home when she said she was going to tell the police if he didn't do so."

"She had never told her husband John, all of the story because there was no reason to do so. She never went out with Homer again."

"What she didn't tell her husband, or anyone else, was that some time after Homer's attempt to rape her she was telling her best friend Kathy Black about Homer trying to rape her and Kathy confessed to her that Homer had indeed raped her and that was why she quit dating Robert."

"Kathy did not report the rape because of the embarrassment."

"Like her husband John, she put Homer out of her mind when Horace was murdered."

"We have not interviewed Homer as of yet. We were going to arrest him as a suspect based on this statement; but he was out of town when we went to pick him up."

"His employer said he was unaware of where

Homer was over the week of the murders he was now on vacation; but another employee at the store, stated that Homer went to Rehoboth Beach for the week."

"Homer Price has been accused of raping a girl in this class when they were in high school and has now been accused of an attempted rape of another girl at the same school. That certainly warrants that we pick him up immediately.

"And by the way, he has a black Toyota sedan and he has a Philadelphia Eagles bumper sticker on his rear bumper. Make a note of that, because a car fitting that description was mentioned of a car parked at Jimmy's Restaurant. That may very well be the car that was seen there in which Horace was seen riding off in. Just perhaps he may have murdered Horace."

"We have a warrant out for his arrest as a suspect in the rape and murder of Jeanne Records, who was raped before she was killed."

"Guys; we have a possible motive on the murders of the women with this accusation against him of two rapes years ago. We must make him a top priority. Let's get him in custody."

"Next on our list to be interviewed was Mary Smoot. Mary is a teller at the Wilmington Trust Bank. She is single but has dated several men occasionally. She stated that she and a friend, Mark Haley, drove to The Flagship Restaurant the night before Horace is thought to have been murdered for a nightcap following a movie."

"When they drove into the parking lot, they saw Horace Hastings and Douglas Weaver having a fight. She said that Horace was getting the best of Douglas as he was a much bigger and apparently a stronger man."

"She said they caught a glimpse of Harriet O'Brien driving out of the lot rather hurriedly. Douglas was bettered in the fight and drove off in his own car. Both Douglas and Harriet left in their own cars so we can presume that they met at the restaurant."

"Mary told us that when they asked Horace what the problem was, Horace told them that when he entered the parking lot Douglas was arguing with Harriet and suddenly grabbed her and began pushing her forcibly into the side of his car."

"They were having a loud and heated argument over something. Then when Douglas hit Harriet, Horace ran over and grabbed Douglas and restrained him from hitting her again. Douglas then started punching Horace but Horace easily got the better of Douglas being so much larger than Douglas."

"She said that Douglas backed off and got in his car and drove off yelling profanity to Horace saying that he would get Horace for that."

"Mary did not know what the argument between Douglas and Harriet was about."

"Gentlemen now we have another motive – a threat that was made to the third murder victim, Horace Hastings who was killed a few days after the women. Douglas was reported as abusing Harriet in the parking lot. Was he angry enough to kill Harriet? Did he follow up on his treat to Horace?

"We have Mary under surveillance for her protection and we also have an arrest warrant out for Douglas Weaver. Let's have him picked up immediately"

"Douglas is reported in Florida at the NASCAR auto races and we will pick him up as soon as he returns. He is with several fellow employees and is in a company car. He should be home late today or tomorrow for sure."

"Our next interview provides a third motive which is a reported pregnancy and concerns about child care and support. Mr. Carle advised me that this motive is one that is often found with the murder of a single woman, second only to sexual attacks."

"The interview was with a girl of the class named Martha Snyder. Martha is divorced and currently lives with a man named George Thompson. George did not attend the reunion with Mary. She stated that she was a close friend of Sally Truitt, another of her senior classmates. Jane told us that Sally got pregnant by a Georgetown, Delaware boy name Alfred Warrington, in her senior year, and left school to have the baby."

"Alfred is the son of a very wealthy lawyer and the grandson of another lawyer equally rich. Martha's statement claims that Alfred's parents had reportedly paid Sally Truitt $150,000 in her senior year at high school to avoid a lawsuit for child support and a college education for the child that Sally demanded."

"Now let's get back to the first victim Harriet. The Coroner's preliminary report stated that Harriet was pregnant but did not report her as being sexually molested."

"Martha said that her best friend Jeanne Records gave her the information about Harriet being pregnant the day before Jeanne was murdered."

"We need to contact the Coroner to determine if he can tell us an approximate date of conception. We may be able to determine who she may have been dating at that time. I do note in the reports that Alfred kept mentioning dates he last dated Harriet. He kept informing us that he had not seen Harriet since March. That was three months before she was murdered. So keep that in mind."

"Alfred seemed to be making certain that we were aware that he had not seen Harriet since March and in his interview he said that March was when he last saw Harriet. Martha wondered if Jeanne had been killed to shut Jeanne up over her knowing about Harriet being pregnant, adding that Alfred may have been afraid of another lawsuit."

"Martha told us that Harriet did not tell her who the father was. In view of Martha's statement, and Alfred's reported connection to Harriet, we then interviewed him. We noticed that he had evidently prepared himself in advance of our interview."

"His responses were quick and appeared to be rehearsed. At least Bill and I got that feeling. He claimed that he had broken up with Harriet in March well before the murders because she was dating others. He claimed that he knew Horace only through his dates with Harriet. He did know Jeanne."

"When you look over these files I just passed out to each of you. I am sure that you will see that we still have a lot of work to do. Bill has told me that he is preparing a list of actions we must take to wrap this thing up, including some interviews that absolutely need to be done immediately. The mayor is on my butt about wrapping this all up.

"Gentlemen, it seems we now have three motives that just might lead us to the killer of these three classmates."

"We will continue interviewing the rest of the class as well as some other people that may put further light on this case. We do need to learn more about that fight at the restaurant parking lot. One of the fighters was our third victim and the other one was accused of hitting the first victim that started the fight."

"That argument could have started inside the

restaurant. Let's contact the restaurant personnel to see if they can give us any input on the argument and hopefully what the argument was about. I also agree with Bill that we need to talk with the Coroner regarding Harriet's reported pregnancy."

"Based on the information obtained in the interview with Fred Dyson in Texas, a second interview with Oliver Hill has been scheduled."

"Our first interview with Oliver stated that Oliver was at home during the days of the murders. There had been nothing to question his statements as no one had even mentioned Oliver Hill in any of the early interviews except two of the earlier interviews had remarks, that he was a strange kid when the class yearbook was shown to those being interviewed. But no one had mentioned him as a possible suspect except Fred Dyson out in Texas. We will interview Oliver again tomorrow."

"We need to follow up on that Georgetown man. I want a team put on each of these three men mentioned in the interviews right away. And let's get the rest of that class interviewed. I am amazed as to what we have found out already. We just have to put it all together somehow."

"We have three suspects at the moment, Homer Price who has been identified as a rapist, Alfred Warrington who impregnated a girl before and paid dearly to settle a lawsuit on child care, and who now has been suggested as possibly having impregnated Harriet, and last we have Douglas Weaver who is said to have threatened Horace who was our third victim, after a fight with him and he was also in a feisty argument with Harriet and had struck her, all of which was just before she was found murdered."

"Have any of you given thought to the fact that we may have more than one murderer involved here?"

Agent Spedden replied, "Well I can't speak for all of us, but I still think we have a single killer, but I must admit I gave thought to that after Mr. Hastings was killed. I was almost certain we had a rapist. I still do and I now have a feeling that Horace was killed simply to throw us all track. I am still fearful that we may have a fourth victim, in Robert Miller. And I also have a strong feeling that he just may be the murderer but we have nothing to support his involvement."

"Just where is Robert Miller. I think we should search the wooded area where we found Horace."

SEVEN

ALL OF THE classmates that were available locally had been interviewed at least two times, except Oliver Hill. He was scheduled for a follow up interview the next day and there had been nothing found that expanded the data already obtained.

There had been nothing to prove proof positive on any of the three suspects, Alfred Warrington, Homer Price, and Douglas Weaver. All three were prime suspects and there was still concern that Robert Miller might have been the killer.

Douglas Weaver was arrested as a possible suspect as soon as he returned from vacation with the death of Horace Hastings because of the threat he was accused of making after his fight with Horace and the fact that he was accused of being seen hitting Harriet O'Brien prior to his fight with Horace. He was also a suspect in the killing of Jeanne but no charge had been made in her murder. The judge refused to release him on bail.

His interview was held in the jail with his lawyer in the room. Douglas was read his rights and was told that he was being charged specifically with the death of Horace Hastings, and also as a suspect on the murder of Harriet O'Brien. There was no mention of Jeanne Records.

Agents Carle and Spedden were conducting the interview.

Agent Carle asked. "Douglas we have several statements that say you were in a heated argument at the Flagship Restaurant with Harriet O'Brien and made threats against Horace Hastings, both of which have been murdered. Is that true?"

"Well I had an argument with Harriet but it was not a heated argument. It was simply over her telling me that she was going to the movies with her friend Jeanne Records and I found her at the Flagship restaurant having drinks and dinner with some other man. It was over her telling me a lie."

"What about your fight with Horace Hastings?"

"It wasn't much of a fight really, I accidentally pushed Harriet in our argument and she fell back against my car and fell to the ground and when I tried to help her up I suppose Horace thought that I was hurting Harriet because he came over and knocked me to the ground. He is a bigger man than I am, so I knew better then to fight him."

"When you left the parking lot, did you make a threat to Horace?"

Doug's lawyer quickly answered for his client, "Don't answer that question Douglas that's incriminating. You don't have to answer that question."

"I have nothing to fear here Mr. Tunnell, I haven't killed anyone. I may have yelled something about his minding his own business; but that certainly was not a threat."

"We were told by a patron in the restaurant that you were using profanity with Harriet even after she told you that the man had just stopped at her booth to talk with her. They said the man just sat down in the booth with Harriet a few minutes before you arrived. They told us Harriet did not come in or eat with the man you saw."

"I don't believe that for a minute. I have been told she was dating another man."

"The manager of the restaurant told you to hold the argument down as you were upsetting the patrons who were having dinner, and that same manger told us that you told him to go to hell. Is that correct?"

"Probably, I was very upset, but at any rate Harriet and I did leave the restaurant and that is when Horace arrived."

"Did you recognize the man that was with Harriet when you went in the restaurant?"

"No, I didn't recognize him but I know that I have seen him somewhere."

"Could he have been a classmate?"

"Possibly, I thought about that, but if he was a classmate of mine, he has really changed in appearance since our school days.

"Can you give us a description of the man? Was he clean shaven, did he wear glasses, color of his hair, you know, something that you are positive about?"

"He did not wear glasses, was clean shaven, was about a foot taller than I am, and of course was a white man. His hair was dark brown and well trimmed but I did notice the way it was combed in the back. What is that you call it, a duck tail or something like that?"

"When I approached the table he had already got up to leave and he smiled and said hello to me and called me by my name. That smile is what really ticked me off. He knew who I was. Harriet probably told him my name when she saw me coming to her booth. That damn smile was to me like he was bragging that he had won Harriet. He was terribly happy about that."

"Doug, we have a copy of your yearbook. If this man called you by name he must have recognized you, we would like for you to take a look at all the pictures of your classmates, possibly that might help you recollect if he was a classmate."

"You will note we have covered the names under the pictures. We want you to possibly recognize a facial similarity of the man you saw with Harriet, without being influenced by a name. I am sure you will recognize most of them."

"The only ones that you probably will not recall are

those that you have not seen in a few years and you have not noticed the gradual change in their appearance. Would you do that for us?"

"Yes, I'll do that. I sure would like to know who that bastard was."

"Why do you call him a bastard? What reason do you have to call him such a name?"

"He was with Harriet and was probably the one she was dating her and caused her to break up with me. I was about to ask Harriet to marry me last March. I had already bought an engagement ring to give to her. Then before I could ask her she broke up with me"

"But the patrons said he only stopped by her table, sat down, and after only being there a short time he got up left. We were told that he did not eat with her. Are you sure he was the man you thought he was?"

"I don't believe that for a minute. There were two dirty plates at the table and two empty bottles of beer. Harriet was surely having dinner with him. If the man you say had paid his bill, surely the table would have been cleared."

"Doug I think that I should tell you again, that one of the restaurant employees told us that Harriet came in first and was seated at the bar waiting for someone, and that when he arrived after a few minutes, they both went to the booth and had dinner and a few drinks. Just as they were finishing their meal another man came in and went to their table."

"The man who ate with her called for the check and

was about to leave when this second man came by the table and shook hands with the first man. The first man left Harriet and the other man still talking and sitting at the table."

"You are correct in what you just said; but the man that came in the restaurant shortly after Harriet was the man she had a meal and some drinks with not the man who joined Harriet as he left."

"It was the second man who was leaving as you came in. So which man were you really arguing with Harriet about, the first or the second?"

"I don't know, but based on what you are telling me, I suppose it was the second, but it really didn't matter because Harriet told me a lie, and that is why I was upset."

"Oh but it does matter Doug, other than yourself, he would have been the last person we know to have seen Harriet alive. Now let's get this straight. The man you described seen with Harriet when you went in the restaurant was actually at, or near the table when you came in. Is that correct?"

"Yes, I saw him at the booth talking to Harriet."

"Ok, then for the record you did not see any other person at the table earlier?"

"No, I only saw the one who got up from the table and left as I approached the booth."

"Ok, now take a look through your yearbook, and see if you can recognize any boy in the book that favors the man you saw that called you by name."

Douglas looked at every picture in the yearbook, and then started to look at them again. He told Carle that he recognized every one of the pictures and that he did not think the man he saw with Harriet was in the book and that he was checking them again to make sure.

On a page in about the middle of the year book, Douglas stopped and spent a minute or so staring at the photograph of Robert Miller. "Yes that could possibly be the man, but I'm not positive.

When told that picture he selected was of Robert Miller. He said. "Oh yes, I haven't seen him in years I knew that I had seen him before. But he's not the man I saw in the restaurant, I saw him in the parking lot he was just getting in his car when I pulled in next to him. He recognized me and called me by my name."

"What else did he say?"

"As best as I can remember he only asked how I was doing and how were things going for me or something like that. I do remember him saying he was in a hurry and that he would try to see me before he went back to the city. After he drove off, I was wondering just who he was."

"Are you certain of that Doug, it's mighty important that you can honestly state that he was the man you saw before going in the restaurant."

"Yes, I will swear to that. I knew that I knew him from somewhere. I do recognize him now although I have not seen him since we graduated. Boy he has really changed. But who was the man in the restaurant?"

"We don't know and we do want to find out. Thank you Douglas you have been a great help and if you can come up with that second man's name I think it just might help to clear you. Start thinking about that it just may save you a lot of problems."

Doug's attorney said, "We will certainly try to determine his name for you. Douglas did not do the things for which he has been charged. I'm going to ask the judge again to release Douglas on bail if necessary. It sounds to me like you are not really sure of his involvement in the murder."

Back at the police station, Agent Spedden told the team, "You know the unidentified man that Doug talks about may just be our murderer. That would not be Robert Miller because Douglas said Miller was outside the restaurant and in his car to leave before he went in the restaurant. Maybe Douglas was right when he said that maybe Harriet was going someplace to meet the man who he saw leaving her table. He may possibly have been the last person to see Harriet alive."

"Yes, but possibly it was Robert Miller she was going to meet. They were all in separate cars as I recall."

"Good logic, add it to the file and send that picture of Miller to our photo lab and tell them to age it by five years. That would certainly account for why he is missing, or he may be the actual killer and wanted to be away from the area. My personal opinion is still that he may have been killed."

"When the art work is back, have the employees and

the manager of the restaurant see if they can pick from a line of pictures the age enhanced photo of Miller."

"But before we jump too fast just who was the second man who stopped and talked to Harriet?"

Agent Carle announced that Alfred Warrington had been arrested and was in jail. His claim of being with his father was found to be untrue when his father denied it under questioning.

Alfred later said that he told them that because of his prior case of paternity he was scared that would surface and point to him because he was with Harriet the night she was probably murdered.

Alfred said that when he was asked where he really was, he had to come up with something quickly. He had hoped his dad would back up his statement but had forgotten to tell his dad about his statement given to the FBI agents.

When Alfred was asked if he had heard that Harriet thought she was pregnant; he said that he did not know that and if she was pregnant it was not his. He claimed he never had sex with her.

When told the second murder victim, Jeanne Records, had remarked to others that Harriet may have been pregnant and he was most likely the father, he again denied the charge.

The Coroner's report, when released, confirmed that Harriet was pregnant and the fetus was three months old. Alfred was dating Harriet by his own admission in March. Alfred had been jailed as a suspect but was released on bail by his parents. His father, a lawyer, told them to get the DNA results.

The next day, the computer generated an aged picture of Robert Miller and it was shown to the Flagship employees and the manager. All of them stated that the photo was the man who ate with Harriet and not the second one that stopped at the booth after he left.

They also stated positively that the second man had been with Harriet many times in the past but he was not the one who had dinner with Harriet the night of the argument.

No one knew who the second man last seen with Harriet was; but they gave a good description of him. He was about 20-25 years of age, was less than 6' tall, and weighed about 175 pounds. He did not wear glasses and had no beard. He was clean shaven. He was a good tipper, and they felt they could identify him if they were shown his picture.

One of the waitresses said she was sure she had seen him in the restaurant several times, but she did not know who he was or who he was with.

A request for photos of all of the suspects was ordered.

EIGHT

OTHER THEN HARRY Black whose whereabouts were still unknown, Oliver Hill was the last of the classmates to be interviewed. Agent Carle met with him at his home.

"Oliver we are doing some follow up interviews with the members of your graduating class and we need to know if you can tell us where you were at the time of Harriet's murder."

"Are you saying that I am suspected of killing that bitch?"

"No. we are just trying to eliminate as many of your class members as we can so we can concentrate on the few suspects we have already. Why would you call her a bitch?"

"Because she was a beautiful girl who used her good looks to get everything she wanted. Unless you were a star football player or someone with lots of money, she stuck up her nose at you. She thought she was a queen or something like that. I am sure she was screwing the entire football team when we were in school."

"Horace Hastings, one of the persons murdered, was a star football player do you think Harriet was messing around with him?"

"I wouldn't doubt it for a minute. Horace married another girl in the class but someone told me that he and his wife were not getting along too well. That's the way it goes when a man gets money. He thinks he can take anything he wants. I know for certain that Harriet and Horace were always good friends. I have seen them together."

"When did you see them together? Do you think Horace had sex with Harriet?"

"Hell yes, I can't prove it but I would bet he had many times. One time I saw her in his car parked in front of Bill Hill's liquor store on old highway 13 while Horace was in the store buying some beer. Horace was in the store when I went in. He said hello to me."

"Can you remember about when you saw them together?"

"I can't remember the exact date but it was several months ago."

"As long ago as March?"

"At least March maybe before that."

"Tell the truth Oliver, did you ever have sex with Harriet?"

"Hell no, I wasn't pretty like her boyfriends and I didn't play sports. She surely would never have let me screw her and I never tried. I've never dated her."

"Oliver, we have been unable to get up with Harry Black. Do you ever hear from him or know where he might be? "

"Harry and I were pretty close friends when we were in school, and I have seen him several times over the years. He and I did some drugs together years ago but Harry couldn't control his use of them. I last saw him here in Seaford a few weeks ago. He spent two nights with me at my house/"

"Are you saying he was in Seaford about two weeks ago? Was that around the time of your reunion??"

"Yes, I met him in a bar on High Street. He was "higher than a kite" for sure. He wanted to borrow some money, I gave him twenty dollars. I don't ever expect to get it back. I had a beer or two with him and he said that he was going to go to the reunion. But of course I understand that he didn't go."

"Did he have anything to say? Did he mention anything about Horace, Harriet or Jeanne? Do you think that he may have raped the girls?"

"Hell no, the last thing in the world Harry and his two friends that were with him, were thinking about was women. All they wanted was more drugs. They had a woman with them. Pretty little thing she was too. He did mention Horace. He said that he understood that Horace was now worth a lot of money, and he did say he might contact him to see if he would loan him some money."

"Do you think he saw Horace or got any money from him?"

"I really don't know if he did or did not because when he left my place with a couple of his druggies they took off for some place. I think, they said they were going to Ocean City at the beach. They were talking about going there in the bar. One of the men with him said he knew a place there where they could get some drugs."

"He said there were sources there for some cheap drugs. When I last saw him that night, he said, I'll see you at the reunion but I never saw him again and of course I did not go to the reunion. I told him I wasn't going to the reunion."

"The two men with Harry may have raped the women but I don't think so. They had a woman travelling with them and she was a hooker. I'm fairly certain they left Seaford after leaving the bar. They were looking for drugs. I know that Harry would not have done that."

"Why do you say that Harry would not have raped the women?"

"Because he's gay that's why. He has no interest in women."

"How about Horace do you think that they could have killed Horace?"

"Well they were all high enough to do something foolish like that, especially if Horace refused to give them drug money. They may have killed him for money. But they were not around Seaford long enough to stay and kill them all. If they did see Horace, I am sure that Horace - would have given Harry some money just as I did. Horace was that kind of guy."

"Horace was not robbed Oliver, he had a lot of money in his wallet when his body was found."

"Well Mr. Carle, if they did it, they sure as hell would not have left any money in his wallet."

The Wilmington police called Chief Daley in Seaford, to report that they had a report from a Mrs. Norman Miller of Wilmington, that her son had not come home or been heard from since he went to Seaford over a week ago and she was inquiring if there was any possibility that the body found in the Seaford Reunion murder, reported in the newspaper, could possibly be her son.

Chief Daley passed the information to Detective Jack Truitt who immediately recognized the name, Robert Miller, as being one of the classmates still reported as missing and who was yet to be interviewed regarding the Seaford reunion murders.

The FBI immediately arranged for an agent to interview Mrs. Miller in Wilmington about 100 miles north of Seaford.

Mrs. Miller told the FBI agent, Charles Wilson that her son Robert had gone to Seaford to meet someone regarding the development of an Internet web address for them.

She said, "Bob graduated from Seaford High School and after he graduated. He had a job offer in Wilmington and I went with him because my husband had passed away. Bob decided to go down and work the account himself and planned to attend his class reunion while in Seaford."

"I have not heard from him for over six days and he almost always called me every day or so. He said it would be nice to see his old classmates again."

"He had not been back to Seaford since we moved to Wilmington when he was hired by the firm where he now works. He is now a partner of the firm."

When asked why she had not reported his failure to come home for so long, she replied," Bob is a very busy man and often went on trips from home for two or three weeks and always contacted her over the weekend. My real concern is that he was not the man found dead in the woods."

They assured her that was not her son. She seemed relieved.

Mrs. Miller said, "Bob has never been away from home over a weekend that he didn't call me and that is why I am inquiring about Robert now. I read about the reunion murders in the paper and that has me worried,"

"Robert did call me and told me that he was in Seaford and had a day playing golf with the men he was working for on Tuesday afternoon. That was two days after he left home. He did tell me he had dinner with one of the girls that he had graduated with, and he was going to look up a girl that he once knew the next morning. I was hoping that was his old girlfriend. Robert has never married. I think he still likes her."

Agent Carle placed a call to Miller's place of business in Wilmington, and a young lady answered the call and arrangements for a meeting with the FBI were made for the next morning.

At the office of Delaware Web Development Company in Wilmington the next morning, the agents found that the company consisted of four people, Robert Miller and Miss Ruth Ferrara and two technicians.. They designed and serviced business web addresses for over 50 companies who were involved with Internet Sales.

Miss Ferrara said Robert was supposed to be downstate working on a very large company that was relocating to Seaford which handled the Internet sales for over a dozen large firms like J C Penny, Sears, Office Depot and others.

Mrs. Ferrara said, "Robert's mother called me just two days ago inquiring about him. I told Mrs. Miller, that I was getting concerned too, as he rarely failed to contact me at least weekly and bring her up-to-date on his progress with the web site."

That evening the local newspaper ran an article about the Class Reunion Murders and reported that another classmate was now missing. They obtained a photo of him from Mrs. Ferrara and included that in the article.

Mrs. Ferrara said that she had contacted the business in Seaford and they said he had been in Seaford, but that they had not seen him for about two weeks. He told them he would be back in about a week with his presentation and that he would be out of state for several days.

Mrs. Ferrara was not overly concerned with Robert being away for so long a time; but she was furious with him for not at least keeping her advised of his progress or what to do with his two weekly pay checks. When he last checked in two weeks ago, he told her he was going to play golf that day with the men he was doing business with.

"Do you know who those men were?"

She told them she didn't know their names. Robert had the file with him.

The FBI got their answer to that question in the afternoon when they received a call from a man named Roscoe Dickens, who told them that he had seen Robert Miller in Seaford, at the DuPont Country Club and her had played a round of golf with a foursome that included Mr. Miller. He added that Mr. Miller mentioned he was planning on going to his class reunion in a few days.

Agent Spedden met with Mr. Dickens and was told, "I went to the golf course to see if I could find anyone to play a round of golf with after breakfast at the club's dining room."

"I do that often, at least two or three times a month, and on this day I met two of my friends who had a guest with them. Their guest was your missing man Robert Miller, and they asked me if I would join them and I did just that."

"During the round Mr. Miller told me that he was in Seaford on business and was creating an Internet web site for the two other gentlemen who owned a large telemarketing firm that processed orders for many nationally known companies such as J C Penny and they were relocating to Seaford after merging their two companies."

"I knew one of them, Norris Borgensen, who also was from Seaford. I didn't know the other gentleman but his first name was Walter."

"After the round of golf, I went into the club's bar and had a beer. Mr. Miller joined me for perhaps thirty minutes or so. He told me that he was from Seaford originally and had graduated from Seaford's high school and that while he was in Seaford he planned to attend his reunion."

"Bob suggested that perhaps we could play a round of golf together again. I told him just give me a call."

"I didn't remember him because he graduated about three or four years after I did. He was younger than I was but I do recall where his parents lived near the school on Fourth Street. I delivered their weekly newspaper."

"They left Seaford while I was out of high school and I remember that their house was vacant for several years before it was finally sold. We boys would go in the back yard and pick pears from a pear tree that was always full of fruit. They were hard as a rock but good eating."

"Then on June 19, I got a telephone call from him and was told that he was back in Seaford and that he would have a free day on the 22nd after the reunion and he wondered if we could get together again for another round of golf. We made plans to meet at the club the morning of the 22nd at 7:30 but he never showed up."

"What was the date that the four of you first played golf together?"

"I'm not sure of exact date, I can't remember; but it was in late May sometime. The second time I saw him was a day or two before his reunion because he told me that is why he was back in Seaford. He did tell me that he was going to meet one of his classmates for dinner that evening and perhaps we could play a round the next morning. That was the last time I saw him. "

"Did he make any remarks to you about any members of his classmates or who he was friendly with while in school?"

"Well now that you mention that, he did ask me if I remembered a girl named Karen, no it was Kathy, Kathy Blake, or something like that.. At the moment I could not think of any such girl with that name but later when I called my wife on the phone I asked my wife if she remembered Kathy Blake she told me that she knew a girl named Kathy who went to live in Virginia with her grandmother."

"When I mentioned that to Robert he said that would probably be the girl he was looking for and that he would ask the girl he was having dinner with that evening, if she knew where Kathy was in Virginia."

"Later that afternoon, my wife called me back on the phone and told me that after she hung up it suddenly occurred to her that I was asking about Kathy Black and not a Kathy Blake. She told me that Kathy was back in Seaford now and that she worked at the Library."

"She had just not made the connection when I called and was asking for a Kathy Blake, not Black. I thought no more of it because I knew he was having dinner with a class mate that evening."

NINE

AGENT CARLE DECIDED to contact Kathy at the library to determine if Robert had discovered that she was back in Seaford and had contacted her or if Harriet had told him that she was back in Seaford.

"Kathy. I am Bill Carle, an agent for the Federal Bureau of Investigation; A few days ago you talked with our agent Bob Spedden, but I am here to talk with you again to see if you can possibly give us some information that may help us bring an end to the murders we are trying to solve."

"We have been told that Robert Miller told someone he knew you from your school days, and he asked about you. He asked if you were still living in Seaford."

"The report states that Mr. Miller was told that you didn't live here, and we wonder if he did learn from someone else who knew you, that you were living and working here in Seaford. Did he eventually get in touch with you?"

"No he did not. I have not seen him since I left Seaford in my senior year although I knew he moved to Wilmington with his mother shortly after his graduation. I had dated Robert many times and I was very fond of him."

"Do you know of any reason why he was inquiring about you? Could he have been upset with any other classmates, and especially those that have been murdered?"

"Mr. Carle, I have no answer as to whether he had any reason to have killed Harriet or Jeanne, but when I read about Horace's death I assured myself that Robert didn't have anything to do with those two murders. But I really wouldn't have been surprised if Homer Price had been killed."

"Why would you be concerned about Homer Price Miss Black?"

"Oh my, I shouldn't have said that. It's a long story Mr. Carle, and a story that I don't want to become known by Robert or my classmates."

"Kathy, if it doesn't have anything to do with these murders, I can assure you that what you tell me will not be made public knowledge, but in honesty to you, if it does have a bearing on these murders, I can only promise you that I will try to keep you out of the headlines. But I feel that you have an obligation to tell us anything that may help us solve these murders."

"Yes, but in a way I will be relieved to finally have

closure on my actions of the past. Please don't open my old case up again. I will still refuse to press charges because I don't want my son to know who his father really is. He has been led to believe his father was killed in an auto accident."

"Kathy, please tell me just what case you are talking about."

"Mr. Carle in my senior year at Seaford High School, I was raped by Homer Price. The Seaford police somehow got wind of the rape, but I denied it because I didn't want Robert Miller to find out about it and because of the embarrassment I would have been faced with."

You don't have to worry about that Kathy, that case is long ago closed and only you can have it opened again. We already knew about Homer. We were told in confidence by another classmate when she was interviewed. Thank you for cooperating with us."

"That would have been Betty Hastings. She is the only person that knows about it. I hope that is has not been told to anyone else."

"It will not be Kathy, but what about my question as to why Robert Miller may have been looking for you?"

"Mr. Carle, Robert and I were the best of friends. We did love each other dearly and were planning on getting married as soon as we graduated in the summer. Then something terrible happened to me."

"Homer Price asked to take me home from a ball game one night when Robert was home with a bad cold. Homer drove me to a wooded area against my will and raped me. I was a virgin and Robert and I had never had sex. I was mortified that if Robert found out that I was raped, he would have been mad enough to do something foolish, maybe even kill him."

"I never told Robert and I don't think he ever knew about it. I made the mistake I guess, by not pressing rape charges against Homer but I was simply too embarrassed to do that."

"There was no way that I would allow that situation to become known because Robert would know that everyone would know that he had married a girl that had been raped."

"I would not allow that to happen. But someone did tell the police, I guess it was Betty, and they approached me and they wanted to arrest the boy that raped me. I would have been happy to see him arrested but I refused to press charges or tell them who raped me. They told me that they did not have his name. I felt that my desire to hide the matter was working."

"At the end of my month, I discovered that I was pregnant. I knew that I would not abort a child, so I talked to my grandmother in Jarrett, Virginia and asked her what I should do. She suggested that I come to Virginia and stay with her and that together we would decide how to handle the situation after that."

"I stayed with her for three years after my son Norman was born. We concocted the story that I had left Seaford to get married, and that we were divorced after we had a child. After my grandmother died I returned to Seaford to live with my parents again. I now have my own home."

"I think it has worked well because everyone I know keeps asking me about the chances of Robert and I getting together again and I tell them that I had changed my name back to Black and wanted nothing to do with him or any man again. I trust that you will help me keep my privacy."

"I promise you that I will never make what you have told me public. I will report simply that you did not see Robert."

"Thank you Mr. Carle."

"Two last questions Kathy, Do you think that Robert was ever made aware of your reason for leaving school."

"Yes and No; Yes, because I wrote him a letter before I left Seaford that I had met another boy and we were going to elope and get married immediately. I told him that I owed him a reason as to why I quit going with him. I simply told him that I loved someone else."

"He never answered that letter, and No because I never told him the real reason. It was because of my love for him that I did not tell him the truth."

"And the last question. Kathy; do you think that Robert may have been led to believe that Horace may have been the person that raped you? That may have given him a motive to kill Horace."

"Absolutely not, I know Bob would never do that without asking me or someone to prove it."

TEN

AGENTS CARLE AND Spedden were at breakfast discussing the cases to date. "Bill, this is all getting quite confusing isn't it?"

"It sure is, We have several suspects for murdering the girls, but it just isn't understood why any of those suspects would have killed Horace other than Douglas who fought with him or now perhaps Bob Miller if he thought that Horace had raped Kathy Black."

"Bill, please don't take this the wrong way, but I can't help but notice that you and Mrs. Hastings are seeing more and more of each other, and with what you told me before about having previously dated each other at college, are you certain that your attraction to her isn't influencing your handling of these murder cases?"

"Isn't Mrs. Hastings a logical suspect? She has more to gain then anyone we know for having Horace killed, and if she thought that he was messing with the two woman isn't that a motive?"

"Well Bob, I must admit that my love for her has definitely been rekindled, but I don't think that I am letting that interfere with my handling of the case. Tell me the truth, do you think that I have done that?"

"Not that I can say but some of the team still think that there is a possibility that Mrs. Hastings may have had something to do with Horace's death because she is the only person that would benefit from his death."

"Oh, I do hope that I am not letting my love for Helen interfere with my duties. I will have to watch that closely. But truthfully I have always had that possibility in the back of my head and I have been wondering just how to handle that."

"One thing that did help me look the other way was the fact; that whoever killed Horace attempted to make it look like a suicide. Certainly Helen would not want to cut herself out of any insurance money by doing that."

"That's true Bill, but whoever did it for Helen, may have wanted us to think it was a suicide hoping to end the search for a killer."

"Maybe so, if there is anything that you or any member of the team thinks that we should explore in that area, please let me know. I do feel that I know Helen well enough to know that she would not do anything like having Horace murdered for money or because of his running out on her, but as we were taught at the bureau you cannot take anything for granted. Helen will most likely inherit a large estate, some day she is an only child and her father is quite wealthy. I don't feel money has anything to do with his murder in so far as Helen is concerned."

"But who I am suspicious of is the man, Larry something who has been advising her how to handle her divorce. Perhaps we should take a closer look at that. Between you and I Bob, don't let the team know just yet, but Helen did give that man $1,500. She said it was for a private investigator to catch Horace in adultery. We will check that out tomorrow. You and I are going to call on that man in Salisbury."

"Yes Bill, I think that would be a great place to start to eliminate Mrs. Hastings' involvement in Horace's death."

"Now back to today's business, I have received the photos I requested of all of the suspects we have. We need to show them to the people at the Flagstaff Restaurant, perhaps we can determine if any of them could be the unidentified man that talked with Harriet after she had dinner with Miller. He would be the last man to have seen Harriet alive. Why don't we slip out there this evening when the waiters and waitresses are there for the dinner crowd?"

Agent Carle and Spedden, showed the photos to all of the employees separately and four of the waitresses identified the photo of Alfred Warrington, as being the individual who quite often had dinner with Harriet. The manager could not identify anyone, but he said he had little contact with the diners. Two waitresses could not identify anyone.

Bill and Bob were having breakfast and going over their notes and discussing what they had. Bob said, "It sure looks like we need to talk to Alfred Warrington again. I'll do that this afternoon."

Carle mentioned, "Homer may have raped and killed the women, but what reason would he have in killing Horace? I am not certain that Douglas would kill anyone. I have the feeling he is just a hothead."

"How about those drug guys that Oliver Hill mentioned, do you think they could be involved?"

"Oliver Hill is the only person that mentioned having seen Harry Black, and if his testimony is true, they are probably not involved. I believe that because as Oliver suggested, they would have taken all the money."

"Well we do have to locate them just to eliminate the questions."

ELEVEN

WORD WAS RECEIVED from the Tampa, Florida, police that Harry Black had been arrested and was in custody. He was charged with selling drugs to minors.

An FBI agent, Charles Carson, out of the Tampa office was instructed to question Harry about his movements from the time he arrived in Seaford, Delaware in June until he arrived back in Tampa.

He was to verify that he was or was not in Seaford, between June 20 when Harriet was reported as having been murdered and June 26 when Horace Hastings was found in a marsh near the Nanticoke River. He was also to be asked about the details of his meeting with Oliver Hill.

"Harry, I understand that you have been charged with selling drugs to a minor15 years old named Kenneth Bronson in Tampa and others. Is that correct?"

"Yes sir, I don't like to sell drugs to kids, but they insisted that I do it or his gang would take them from me by force. I didn't want to be hurt, so I sold them some of my own drugs."

"The police say that you sell to kids all the time."

"They lie. I sell only when I am about to be beat up."

"I have a report here that says you sold some drugs to a kid up in Seaford, Delaware is that true?"

"No, that is not true I sold some up there to a man who was a friend of mine, but not to any kids. I needed some money."

"What was the kid's name?"

"I told you he was not a kid he was a man of my own age. I went to school with him. His name is Oliver Hill. He and I did drugs many times in high school, ask him and he will tell you that. He is not a kid."

"If you do sell drugs, why don't you like to sell to children?"

"That's easy. The police really get up tight when drugs are sold to kids. If we sell to adults they don't really care. I guess they think the older people are already hooked on drugs or should know better than to use them."

"Are you hooked on drugs Harry or just involved with selling them?"

"I guess that I'm hooked on them again. I'm going to ask the judge to place me in rehab again. I sell only to pay for my own habit."

"Have you been in rehabilitation for drug abuse before?"

"Yes, several times. I stop every once in a while but it seems I just can't do without them and I wind up back on the streets selling again every time I get clean. If I could find a job I think I could kick the habit."

"When you were in Seaford were you using drugs when you sold to the kids?"

"Damn it, I told you I didn't sell any drugs to any kids in Seaford. It was only to a man my own age. Oliver Hill like I just told you. Ask him, or ask the men I was with in Seaford, they will tell you. Oliver was with us for an evening in a bar. He gave us money and we gave him some pot."

"OK I will ask all of them. Maybe that would help your case when you are sent up there for questioning. Who were the two men with you?"

"What do you mean – when I am sent up there? Just why am I going to be sent to Delaware."

"I'll explain that to you later, just for now, answer my questions."

"They are both from Ocean City, Maryland and here in Tampa when it gets cold up north.. I was in Ocean City with them, and they went with me to Seaford, because I gave them some drugs to take me over there so I could attend my class reunion."

"My girlfriend was off in her van. Their names are Johnnie James and Henry Walker. They live in Ocean City, Maryland in the summer on the road to Fenwick

Island, Delaware but they are here in Tampa most of the time."

"Ocean City has a lot of drug dealers there in the summer, that is why we were there, but in the winter its' like a ghost town. Ask the guys in Ocean City and they will confirm what I am telling you."

"Ok, we will. You said your girlfriend was off with her van. It says here that you are thought to be gay."

"I am gay. The girl travels with me. She's a hooker. She keeps the two of us in drugs. She owns the van we travel in. Most of the time we just sleep in it too."

"Did you sleep in it when you went from Tampa to Delaware?"

"No because there were four of us. We shared a motel room most of the time. In Seaford we stayed at my friend Oliver Hill's house."

"What was the girl's name?"

"Grace Marvel, she's from Baltimore. She really likes Johnny James."

"Who's Johnny James?"

"He's one of the two men that went to Seaford with me."

"Oh, yes I remember you said that. Did you get to your class reunion?"

"No, I got stoned and I decided not to go. The only reason that I wanted to go anyway was to see my old buddy Oliver Hill. I spent two days with him before the reunion and he brought me up to date with the people I knew."

"In fact he told me that one of the girls in the class had been raped the day after I arrived and he jokingly asked me "You didn't rape her did you? I told him that he knew better than that. Oliver knows that I 'm gay."

"Oh, how would he have known that?"

"Oliver was my lover in high school, but don't tell him I said that."

"Was Oliver gay too?"

"No, he's as straight as an arrow; but he was so ugly, none of the girls would have anything to do with him. I was his solution."

"Sometimes I would take him to see some girls I knew who were on drugs. They would do it for drug money in spite of his looks. Boy he is one ugly guy. One of his eyes was bigger than the other and it bulges out. He wears dark glasses most of the time now to hide them. But he is a good friend of mine. We used to play sometimes in a band for money."

"Back to when you were in Seaford Harry -- you said that Oliver told you about a girl named Harriet O'Brien that had been found raped the day after you arrived. Did he tell you that she was murdered?"

"Oh yes, he did tell me that, but all he said about it was that she had been raped and strangled to death. Wait a minute; you don't think I had anything to do with that do you? Is that why you are questioning me about Harriet? And why you said I was to be sent up there?

"No, Harry, I am rather certain that you didn't do it but we must question everyone that knew Harriet, I need to show my boss some evidence that you were not in Seaford, when she and the other woman were murdered. You just told me that you were in Seaford the day before Harriet was killed. That would put you in Seaford on the June the 19th. On what date did you leave Seaford?"

"I was in Seaford at Oliver's house just one night on that trip. That would have been June 20th when I left. You mean there were other murders besides Harriet?"

"Yes, there were two others. Another woman named Jeanne Records, and a man named Horace Hastings. Did you know them and can you think of any reason all these people were murdered?"

"Oh no, Jeanne was such a nice girl. She was Harriet's best friend in high school. They were like two peas in a pod. They were always together. If Harriet was murdered, and anyone knew why or who did it Jeanne, would be the one to ask. If they were still as close as they were in school, I would bet that she knew why Harriet was killed. Perhaps she was killed to keep her from telling."

"Any thoughts on why Horace was murdered?"

"Horace was a very popular guy and a star athlete. He was a great football player. He was also a nice guy. I can't believe that anyone would want to kill him? I can't count the many times that he sat down with me and tried to get me to stop doing drugs and then after lecturing me he would give me some money knowing that I was going to get more drugs. I should have listened to him."

"Did he give you any money when you were in Seaford?"

"No; I didn't get to see him at all. My friends were anxious to get back to Ocean City after we sold some drugs in Seaford and in Dover while I was staying at Oliver's house."

"Tell me what you know about Robert Miller. He has been reported as missing."

"I don't remember too much about Bob Miller. He seemed to be a nice guy, but I never had too much contact with him. I do remember him in the 12th grade he always seemed upset about something and quit going to the football and basketball games and rarely participated in any school activities. I think he had a chip on his shoulder."

"I know he left Seaford, but I can't remember if he graduated with us before he left or not."

"Yes he did graduate with you, but he moved to Wilmington, Delaware shortly after he graduated. Somebody said that he left because he was heartbroken over some girl."

"Oh yes, I remember that now. He was voted as the guy who would be the first to get married in the class. But such was not the case because his girl friend, Kathy quit dating him, quit school, and married somebody down south."

"Did you by chance see Robert when you were in Seaford?"

"No, but Oliver Hill told me that he saw him at the Flagship Restaurant with a woman."

"Did he tell you who the woman was?"

"I don't remember if he did or not, yes he did, I remember now, Bob was with Harriet O'Brien. They were having dinner. Oh gosh, I hope Bob didn't kill Harriet."

"Did Oliver say who he was with at the Flagship Restaurant?"

"Not that I can remember, oh wait, I do remember him telling me that he had sold his old pickup truck to a used car salesman, and after he signed the old title, he had a beer with him. That's who it was."

"Do you know the name of the car salesman?"

"No, I have no idea."

"Thank you Harry, I hope that you can stay clean this time. Everyone said that you had a lot of musical talent."

"I'm going to try. Believe me Mr. Carson; I had nothing to do with those murders."

"I'm sure you didn't Harry. I'll see what I can do to help you in Delaware, but I can't help you on these Florida charges."

After the interview was over agent Carson called agent Carle in Delaware and told him all the information that Harry had given him and promised to fax the transcript as soon as it was typed.

"Bill, I don't believe Harry Black was in Seaford after those two days he was staying with Oliver Hill, and he told me that he had stayed in a motel in Ocean City, Maryland on June 19 the night that Harriet was last seen at that party. I confirmed with the motel that he had been in Ocean City on June 20th."

He was in a motel in North Carolina on the night of June 24 that Jeanne was determined to have been raped. That indicates to me that he was on his way back to Florida during that period."

"Of course there is a possibility; he may have gone back to Seaford after June 20. He could not tell me where he was each night because he was full of drugs and he had made two or three trips to Dover from Oliver's house. His answer was that he knew he went back to Oliver's house because he had left his girlfriend with Oliver in return for some money and he picked her up.. He said his girl was a prostitute."

"He had people with him and they didn't want to wait for him to go to the reunion so they decided to go back to Florida."

"There were three passengers with him, a girl and the two male addicts that we talked about before. He told me the girl owned the van they were traveling in and that she was also addicted o drugs."

"I would suggest that you look into what he said about why the Records girl was murdered. That seems logical to me. He could not give me any suggestions on why Hastings was murdered."

TWELVE

THE INVESTIGATION SHIFTED from Harry Black back to the other suspects Alfred Warrington, Homer Price and now Oliver Hill. The team was instructed by agent Carle to focus on possible reasons why Horace Hastings was killed.

"Douglas Weaver certainly had a motive to kill Horace because of his rage after their fight, but is there a possible connection between Horace and the two women that would result in Horace's murder, or is there still another reason."

"I don't think that Douglas had anything to do with the murders or rape of the two women. I wish that DNA report would get here soon. It may give us the answers we need. We need to work with the forensic people and see if there is a possibility that Horace may have killed himself in spite of the evidence that proves he did not."

The forensic report eliminated the possibility that Horace had killed himself. It reported that he was shot in the back of the head and the trajectory of the bullet indicated that it would have been impossible for the victim to hold the gun in that position and the bullet from the gun at his side when his body was found was not a match to the one that killed him. Suicide was now out of the question completely.

"So with a suicide out of the picture just where are the connections? It is still a puzzle that has to be resolved. Is there a possibility that the three were not murdered by the same person? It is now my opinion that there are two murderers on the loose? Could we have overlooked the real killer of Horace, or the women?"

"Let's do another round of interviews. There has to be an answer that we have over looked. Jack, I would like for you to work on Harriet O'Brien."

"Bob you are to work on Jeanne Records."

"I will concentrate on Horace Hastings"

"And gentlemen agent Walter Roadermel from our Wilmington office has joined us today. He will concentrate on tying all the transcripts together for our daily briefings, and see if there are any discrepancies in the interview transcripts."

"The mayor is anxious to bring a suspect on these murders to trial. If necessary, we can prosecute each murder separately. If we can prove a killer for any one of the victims let's proceed that way. The public is getting weary that we have not yet identified a killer."

"But at least, now that we have a suspect, Douglas Weaver in jail the class members are talking more freely."

"The mayor says the Attorney General informed him that we will not have to wait to prosecute a killer for all the victims at the same time. If we have a good case on a single murder, he feels that a trial may bring to life something that we are missing and may give us the connections we have been unable to make."

"Jack we know that Alfred Warrington lied to us by telling us he was in Dover at the time of Harriett's death. What do you think about charging him with the murder of Harriet O'Brien and bringing him back in for prosecution? He is out on bail now"

"Bill, I would hope that we wait just a little longer, please give me just a little more time to verify his actual whereabouts and to expand on a few interviews of the class members in which Alfred was mentioned before we charge him."

"OK, Jack I was hoping that you would say that, I don't feel that we have the proof we will need in court so we will wait before making a charge. I am hoping that if we can just get one of these suspects in court and everyone knows that they are in jail; just perhaps, someone who may have information but has been afraid to tell us about it out of fear, just may contact us."

"Chief, the classmates are all still very afraid. I think we may just strengthen our case against Alfred or at least possibly solidify the connections we have between the three murders. No jury will ever convict him on what little evidence we have. We need the DNA."

"No problem Jack, I think you have a good point. We should not rush into anything until we get the DNA but maybe someone in the class may be afraid to talk without knowing that the real killer is indeed locked up as you suggest."

"I will ask the prosecutor that we pick up Homer Price on a rape charge. Homer certainly is a strong suspect on the murder of Jeanne Records based on our interview with Kathy Black. I will ask Kathy to let us make the charge so that we cannot let that crime go unpunished and to keep him from doing it again."

The next morning the Wilmington Morning News carried the headlines that Jack was hoping for. "***Second man arrested in the Reunion Murders***. The article went on to say that Homer was a suspect in the murders of Harriet O'Brien and Jeanne Records. It made no mention of the rape of Kathy Black.

Also written in bold type was what Jack, was really wanting. "***He is confined in the Seaford jail.***"

Jack's theory was working by the end of the day the police had four telephone calls from four different class members who stated that they had some input into the case against Alfred Warrington

The first to call was Bernice Titus., a neighbor of Horace Hastings. She asked for Chief Daley. Chief Daley talked with her and heard her reason for the call.

After Chief Daley assured her that what she had to say

would never be revealed to anyone as having been made by her she began to talk freely.

"My children and the children of Horace and Helen Hastings play together and I just don't want to get involved in this mess but I have some information that just might have a bearing on Horace's death."

"Mrs. Titus, I want to thank you for calling us and telling us that you have additional information that may have a bearing on the case. As you said it may have a bearing on the death of Horace Hastings, I am going to transfer your call to FBI agent William Carle, who is working specifically, at the moment, on the death of Mr. Hastings."

"I can assure you that your report will be held in strict confidence. I do appreciate your call and if it will help us in solving these murders, the public will be relieved and then we get back to some normalcy in this city. Hold on and I will transfer you now. Thanks again."

"Agent Carle, how may I help you?"

"Mr. Carle I would like to tell you something that may have a bearing on the death of Horace Hastings. If you are already aware of what I will tell you, please let me know."

"That's great Mrs. Titus. Would you prefer that I come out to take your statement or would you prefer to do it here on the telephone?"

"I would feel better if we could talk privately at my home. Does your car have any markings on it to indicate that you are from the police or FBI?"

"No, the car that I would come in has no markings and I am sure that no one would know that you were talking to us. Would you give me directions to your home and a time to meet with you?"

"Mr. Carle, you have been near here before. I live on the next farm just past Horace Hastings' farm. Our farm is on the same side of the road as Horace's farm. Our house is a green two story house and our name Titus is painted on our mail box. I will be at home all afternoon. I wouldn't want Mrs. Hastings to know about our conversation."

"Oh yes, I have seen that house, I know where you live I can be there promptly at 2:30 today if that is OK."

"Yes that will be great. My husband will not be home, but he is aware of what I wish to talk to you about?"

"Great, I will see you at 2:30. I will be in a dark green colored 4 door Ford automobile. I will see you then."

Promptly at 2:30. Agent Carle knocked on the door of Henry and Bernice Titus. Mrs. Titus answered the door and welcomed him inside.

"Mrs. Titus, before we start I have to, advise you of your rights and to make you aware that I will be taping your statement. Is that understood?"

Yes I understand."

"Please state your name and the date and then begin.'

My name is Bernice Titus and the date is July 14, 1989. Mr. Carle, my husband and I would like to bring to your attention a matter that may have a bearing on the reason Horace Hastings was murdered."

"We do not know if anyone has told you this before or not; but again if they have, just let me know and we can close the conversation."

"I understand Mrs. Titus please go on with your statement."

"It is really more of an observation than a statement. I know that Horace and Helen had not been getting along with each other for some time now."

"At the reunion they did not even sit at the same table. I understand that she has filed for a divorce. But from what I hear; it should be Horace that should be filing for a divorce because Helen is the one seeing another man."

"I don't know his name but I have seen Helen meet him in town and then go off with him in his car. Horace will not give her a divorce unless she gives him the children. Helen told me that herself."

"Did you know that this was going on in the Hastings household? My husband and I figure that this individual may have something to do with Horace's death and perhaps Horace was killed for his money or to obtain custody of their children. A lot of us think it might."

"Mrs. Titus, you just mentioned, a lot of us, who are the "us" people you mention?"

"A lot of our classmates, after the reunion when Horace's death was reported, everyone was talking about Horace and Helen. We are thinking that Harriet may have been killed because she was messing with Horace and that Horace may have been killed by this same man for money. I have seen him one several occasions with Helen. We think he was killed for his money. He was probably killed over money or over child custody."

"Horace loved those two kids of his and I'm sure he would have done anything to keep from losing them. And at the same time, Helen would probably do the same over them. Some of us even went so far as to suggest that Helen hired a killer to eliminate the two women that Horace was seeing, and then to kill her own husband to get all his money and full custody of the children."

"To my knowledge, Mrs. Titus, we have not been advised of this situation, and it is certainly something that we will have to follow up on. Tell me do you have any idea where we could get the name of this man you say she is seeing?"

"No, I have no idea who he is or where we can get that information, but my husband said that he had Maryland tags on his car."

"When Helen told me that she and Horace were at odds with one another; she admitted to me that she was seeing another man to help her win a divorce settlement that would help her get permanent custody of her children all the time. She didn't want Horace to have any custody rights at all because she didn't want the children exposed to his lifestyle. He didn't look like a lawyer to me."

"I asked her who he was and she simply said you don't know him he's from Salisbury, Maryland."

Agent Carle underlined Salisbury, Maryland. He

remembered Helen telling him about the man she had engaged to help her with her divorce, a man named Larry Adams.

"Do you know if Horace knew about the man?"

"I don't know about that but Horace thought that she was cheating on him because he told my husband that he caught her with a man in a restaurant having dinner and he was going to use that to get custody of the children. It may have been the same man."

"Thank you Mrs. Titus, we appreciate your making us aware of this information. It may possibly help us find our murderer. Can you suggest some names of Mrs. Hastings very closest friends who possibly might have more information on Mrs. Hastings new male friend? Is your husband aware that you are giving us this information?"

"Yes he is aware that I was going to call you. As for Helen's close friends; both Jeanne Records and Harriet were two of her very closest friends but they are both dead as you know. That is one reason that I decided to call you. Probably Susan Hill or Thelma James might be the two who are also close to her. In fact Thelma was the first to tell me Helen was cheating on her husband. She saw then together at the Flagship restaurant having lunch."

"Thanks again, by chance would you have their telephone numbers or how their number would be listed in the telephone book?"

"Let me go get the telephone directory and I will give you their numbers."

Back at the police station, Chief Daley called for a

special meeting of the team and gave them a report of the information that Mrs. Titus had told to agent Carle.

There was a lot of discussion as several on the team had already questioned if Helen may have had something to do with Horace's death and possibly the women as well."

"Men, I feel that we now need to explore this suggestion that Mrs. Hastings or this stranger friend of hers may have something to do with Horace's death."

"We certainly have a valid reason why he may have been killed. If this love triangle is; in fact, the reason for Horace's being killed then the question now is who actually killed him."

"Could his wife Helen have actually killed him or had him killed? She certainly was not the killer of the women, Jeanne was sexually abused."

"She certainly had two reasons for having him dead, both money and child custody. Could this boyfriend of hers be the killer of Horace?"

Agent Carle, asked to make a statement, "Chief Daley, men, I have a scheduled meeting with Mrs. Hastings at 3:30 this afternoon to discuss those very possibilities that Chief Daley just made."

"I am anxious to find out just who this so-called boyfriend is. I know she will tell me. I will then make plans to interview him tomorrow morning and have Bob will be with me."

"I know that several of you are aware that Mrs. Hastings, Helen, is a long time personal friend of mine since our college days. Bob and I have already discussed the very suggestion the chief just mentioned, and men I can promise you that my relationship with Helen, will in no way, interfere with my proper handling of her possible involvement. I will have a full report for you all after my interview with the man tomorrow. This interview will be at his place of business in the morning and will be unannounced."

"Bill none of us, including myself as chief, have any doubts on your proper handling of these cases. We know that you will not allow personal matters interfere with your responsibilities. We are anxious to hear your report on this friend of Mrs. Hastings. We hope that you will get a favorable report and hopefully some information that might help us find Horace's killer."

"Thank you chief, I am thinking that this so called boyfriend may provide us with the missing link that we need to tie all of this together. He himself would stand to gain from Horace's death if he married Helen. He may feel that Helen would eventually marry him. We have to find out just what kind of a man he is. Is he after her money, or is he a hired killer, or is he simply a friend? I intend to find out."

"I am getting a strong gut feeling that Horace's murder may have no connection what so ever to the deaths of Harriet or Jeanne, and their deaths may only have given the murderer of Horace a chance to divert suspicion away from himself. I remember suggesting this very thought some week or so ago."

"The fact that many people do know about the Hastings' marital troubles; I suggest we go back and question her about that. I will be out there later today. Agent Spedden will go with me."

"I have two names that Mrs. Titus gave me as close friends of Mrs. Hastings, and I will interview both of them today before we go see Helen if I have time. I still need to confirm the name and where to find him of Helen's so called boyfriend and anything about him that may tie him to the murder. Hopefully we will have that information when we talk to Helen so we can follow up on it tomorrow with him."

"I hope to obtain more information on all these revelations. I am sure we are on the right track in so far as Horace's death is concerned. I have to remember that Mrs. Hastings might indeed have a part in the murder even though I am rather sure she did not."

THIRTEEN

AFTER IDENTIFYING HIMSELF as an FBI agent, an arrangement to speak with Thelma James in private at the clothing store where she worked was authorized by her manager. Agent Carle was given permission to talk with Thelma.

"Mrs. James, I have been told that you are a close friend of Mrs. Horace Hastings. Is that true?"

"Yes. Mr. Carle, I consider her as a very close friend and I think that I am perhaps one of her closest friends too."

"Great. Then perhaps you can help us with a few questions that we have regarding her relationship with her husband at the time of her husband's death. I wonder if you can tell us what you know about that relationship. We feel that if anyone would know you may be the one that could possibly advise us of that relationship."

"Well, I want you to know first that Helen, Mrs. Hastings, and I are in the same bridge club and we rode together wherever we were to play, once every two weeks, and have done that for years. I go by her house and pick her up almost all the time. Several times, she would drive to my house and pick me up."

"We have shared a lot of information over the years during our rides together as well as at our bridge games. What you probably are looking for is information on Helen and her husband's divorce problems."

"Yes, that is one of my questions. What problems were they facing over the divorce?"

"There were a lot of problems. Helen told me that Horace was cheating on her and that they had not lived as man and wife for well over a year. I asked who the woman was, and she said that she did not know for sure, but she thought it was Harriet O'Brien."

"They still lived under the same roof, because of the children but Helen told me that he rarely came home anymore. She thought he was staying on his boat. He has a big boat down near the ocean somewhere."

"The main problem with their divorce settlement was that Horace would not agree to Helen's request that he agree to give her full time custody of their two children. She was willing for him to have visitation rights but no custody. She told me that she would be willing to negotiate a money settlement."

"About five or six months ago, she had arranged for a business man that was introduced to her as someone that could help her with her divorce. As I understood it, he had successfully won a divorce from his own wife and did get full custody of his child."

"I don't know his full name, but his first name is Larry and I know that he lives in Salisbury, Maryland."

"Now, you probably have heard that Helen was having an affair with Larry, but I know that is not true. Helen told me, and I believe her, that he was only a friend that was helping her. She did say that he was a nice man and that she enjoyed his company and trusted his advice."

"She said that they have had several dinners together to discuss matters of the divorce; but they had not done that in the last month or so, because she found out that Horace was telling his attorney that she was having an affair with Larry, so that he could accuse her of adultery."

"Mr. Carle believe me when I yell you this, if you have heard about her having an affair, those accusations are all lies, and they were being spread by Horace himself. He wanted her to appear as an adulterer."

"Mrs. James, I have learned a long time ago, to work only with confirmed information. We listen to both sides of all disputes and have learned how to determine who is telling the truth. We have ways of doing that."

"I do thank you for this information. It just may help us get to the bottom of these murders. Can you tell us your thoughts on Jeanne Records and give us any information on her that may have been a motive that led to her death?"

"All that I know about Jeanne was that she was a close

friend of Harriet also. Perhaps she knew why Harriet was killed. I did hear that Horace was seeing Jeanne at times, but I have never seen them together except the night of the reunion they did a lot of dancing together."

Agent Carle next found Susan Hill at home and arranged to interview her there that afternoon.

Mrs. Hill, I have been told that you are a close friend of Mrs. Horace Hastings. Is that true?"

"Yes. I am, I consider her as a very close friend and I am sure that I was one her closest friend too before all this mess started."

"What mess are you talking about Mrs. Hill?"

"I mean since she started running out on her husband. She has two young children and a nice husband. He has plenty of money, and I just can't figure out why she would do that."

"Can you tell me how you know she was running out on her husband and how you know that to be a fact?"

"Well, Horace told me himself, when I asked him at the reunion who that man was with his wife at her table. He told me she was her new lover."

"She introduced the man to me merely as a friend. Horace was also at the reunion, but he was alone. Helen sure made Horace feel embarrassed when she arrived with that man."

"Horace then told me of his problems and said she was trying to get full custody of their children. He said that she was claiming that he was committing adultery, but it was Helen that was doing the cheating."

"I think that Helen married Horace for his money and was trying to get it all away from him. I have never heard of Horace running out on his wife."

"I wouldn't be surprised if she didn't hire someone to kill him."

"Well we have been told that Horace often dated her in high school. Then in his junior year at college they were married, he was certainly not a man of wealth at that time. We also understand that it was Helen's parents that gave Horace the money to start his poultry business. I have been told her parents are very wealthy and she is an only child. Is that true?"

"Yes, I guess that is right. I take back what I just said about her marrying him for his money. But, I still think she was doing the running out."

"Thank you Mrs. Hill. Can you tell us of any reason why Harriet O'Brien or Jeanne Records were murdered or of any connection with either of them to Mrs. Hastings?"

"I think that Helen had her husband killed. I have nothing to back that up, but any woman who would run out on her husband with two lovely young children might do anything. Then there's the money that probably falls into the truth of what really happened."

"I can't imagine why the two women were killed. That probably had nothing to do with Horace's murder because they were raped."

"Only Jeanne Records was found to have been raped Mrs. Hill."

"Oh, I didn't know that. Jeanne was always a close friend of Harriet every since school days. That is the only connection that I can think about them having. Maybe Harriet knew who raped Jeanne."

"No, that would not be right Jeanne was murdered after Harriet was. Harriet would not know that Jeanne had been raped."

"Oh dear, yes that's right, I need to stop and think all of this over again."

"Yes, do that Mrs. Hill, and if you can think of any connections, or hear anything that may have a connection to these murders, please do contact us at the Seaford Police Station."

FOURTEEN

AGENTS CARLE AND Spedden arrived precisely at 3:30 in the afternoon as arranged by telephone earlier with Mrs. Hastings.

"Helen, we do hate having to talk with you about Horace's death again but something has come to our attention that only you can help us with. We have just learned that you have been seeing a man. Is that true?"

"Bill I thought I told you about that. It is true that Horace and I have been at odds now for well over a year and we were close to reaching a settlement. We were just far apart with an argument over the care and custody of the children. I am sure that I already told you that."

"Not everything Helen, we learned a lot more just today, and it is this new information that has opened up an entirely new approach for us; and that is the possibility that Horace may have been killed because of your marital differences."

"Wait a minute Bill, you don't think for a minute that I killed Horace or had him killed do you?"

"No we are not saying that Helen, but it does create a possibility that his death was as a result of your marital difficulties."

"Our team has wondered who would gain by the death of Horace and it does points to you, your boyfriend, or Horace's own family as being logical suspects."

"Wait a minute Bill, I have no boyfriend you should know that by now. Who are you referring to as a boyfriend?"

"We have been told that you have been seen having dinner several times with a man from Salisbury, Maryland. Is that true?"

"Bill, I thought you were aware that I had a friend helping me with my divorce. I suppose you are referring to Larry Adams, because he is the only man that I have had dinner with since my marital troubles started, except you of course."

"I have heard that accusation before. Other then at the reunion, and our first several meetings when I asked him to help me with my divorce, I have not been with him at all. He is definitely not a boyfriend or anything like that."

"He's a business man in Salisbury that was referred to me by a friend of mine who lives in Salisbury to assist me in making certain that I got full custody of the children and was not cheated out of my part of our money in the divorce. I told you about him when we first talked about all this weeks ago. He is certainly not a boyfriend."

"I will need money to educate and provide for my two children. I don't want to be in a position to ask my parents for help. Horace's business was funded in a major part by my family. I think I told you that my dad gave us $50,000 to build those chicken houses. There would have been no wealth, if we had not had that loan and his cosigning some notes at the bank for us."

"Mr. Adams said that I was entitled to a share of the business because of that loan and promised to help me get it in a divorce settlement."

"Helen, Horace's death would have cleared the way for what we were led to believe was a boyfriend to gain financially by marrying you, and Horace's death would open that door. There was even talk that perhaps he killed Horace for you."

"Bill, I certainly hope that you do not think that is true and I can assure you that Larry and I will never get married. I have absolutely no interest in him in that area. I hardly know the man."

"I also hope that he does not think that way about our relationship and to be truthful, I wanted to make sure that I was being advised properly, by having made an appointment with a lawyer, Henry Faulkner, of Laurel to represent me in this matter."

"Have you told Mr. Adams about that?"

"Not yet, I was about to do that when Horace was killed, but you can check on that with Mr. Faulkner."

"Well Helen, we are here now because we would like to check out the possibility that he had plans on marrying you to get to Horace and your money. He may have been thinking along those lines even if you were not. Would you give us his business name, where he lives, and tell us what you know about him?"

"I will give you what you want to know; but I can promise you that he did not kill Horace. His name is Larry Adams, and he lives in Salisbury, Maryland. He owns an auto repair shop Adams Auto Repair Shop on The road to Ocean City in Salisbury and he is financially sound."

"He would not need Horace's money and beside that most of our money would be in trust for our children anyway. Horace and I had agreed on that much already. Larry is divorced and is a prominent businessman in the city. He is even a member of the Wicomico County Commission."

"Did he ever ask you about marriage?"

"No, at least not directly, it is true that Larry had hinted at a relationship, but I was in no rush to get involved with any man and least of all to get married and I had told him that."

"He once asked me if I would be interested in just living with him, and of course I told him no way, but I did tell him that I would not live with any man unless I was married to him and I definitely was not ready for that."

"Are you saying that you and Mr. Adams have never discussed the possibility of marriage other than by what you just told me?"

"Absolutely not, I hope he didn't get that impression. He did mention a relationship once or twice; but he has never actually asked me if I would marry him. If you are wondering if we ever had sex the answer is absolutely not."

"He was aware of the status of our divorce because I was asking him for advice. He was already divorced and knew how a divorce works. He was helping me to make sure that I was not cheated. He gained custody of his children and that is hard for a man to do. That is why he was referred to me. He had been through a custody battle himself."

"Did he know that a trust would get most of the proceeds set up for the children?"

"No, I never mentioned that to him but he did suggest that I should make sure that some of the money should always be readily available for the children's needs and not locked up in a trust should I need any for their education and support. He told me that should be stated in the divorce agreement."

"Can you tell us how the divorce was to handle your farm and its' business. It appears that the bulk of Horace's estate would be in the poultry operation itself?"

"Yes, that is true, and that is where we were having our difficulty in reaching an agreement on the divorce. Horace didn't want to get rid of any of his farm property or the poultry business and I argued that my parents were the ones that gave us most of the money when we needed it to build the chicken houses; and that I, in a sense, was a partner in that business. I had signed several notes to get the bank loans we needed. They are now all paid off."

"Did Mr. Adams make any suggestions on how to handle that problem?"

"Yes he did, he suggested two ways to handle that. One was to determine if Horace's brothers and father were interested in buying me out of the business entirely and the other suggestion he made was for Horace to cash out the cash value of a life insurance policy he had and have the funds paid to me in exchange for my half of the business."

"Was the policy's cash value, large enough to do that?"

"He thought so. We bought it when we were really up to our ears in debt when we built the broiler houses and equipped them. The bank and my father insisted that we buy the policy before they would loan us the money."

"The policy was for a million and a half dollars but when Larry contacted the insurance company, he said I would have gotten only a little over one hundred thousand dollars and that was only if the policy was amortized over forty years rather than being cashed and he advised me not to accept that. I agreed with Larry I would not accept that."

"One last question, I can't recall if we asked you on your first interview or not, but can you tell me exactly where you were the night that Horace was killed? We have to ask that question on every person being interviewed."

"Well I am not certain which night he was killed. He did not come home at all on two nights before he was found. On the first night I was over to my friend Thelma James' house playing bridge with our bridge club, and on the second night I was at home with my children. I think that is correct."

"Oh, one last question. Did Larry Adams ever ask you for any money?"

"Only once, he said he needed five hundred dollars to pay a lawyer to research the titles to our properties and one thousand dollars to pay a private investigator to obtain proof that Horace was committing adultery."

"Did you give him the fifteen hundred dollars?"

"Yes, I did in cash."

"Did you ever get a report from that private investigator?"

"No not yet. I don't know if he made a report to Larry or not."

"Thanks again Helen. We will be talking with Mr. Adams tomorrow. Helen, please do not contact him and let him know we will be talking to him. It is very important that we meet with him when he does not know that we will be asking him questions in advance. I ask that you don't contact him for your own security."

"I promise you Bill that I will not contact him at all. I have an attorney now helping me with my problems from now on. I think I told you that. His name is Henry

Faulkner; his office is in Laurel, Delaware. Oh, I think I told you that already. Bill tell me the truth, do you think Larry had anything to do with Horace's death?"

"Helen, the only thing that I can honestly tell you for certain is that he may have. We are of the opinion that he had reason to do so and we will have an answer to your question very soon."

On their way back in town, both the agents commented that they were certain that Horace had been murdered for money and they felt that this Larry Adams was now a prime suspect.

They felt that he seemed to be using Helen in an attempt to gain access to Horace's estate through a relationship or marriage to her. He was probably well aware what Helen's monetary interest in Horace's estate would be. His guilt would also explain why the scene was made to look as a suicide but poorly staged knowing that it would be proven not a suicide and that the proceeds of the insurance policy would have to be paid to Helen and that the divorce case would be closed.

The death of Horace would certainly bring a lot of cash into the estate and a marriage to Helen would give Larry access to that. They were certain that Larry had a reason to benefit from Horace's death.

Agent Carle told Bob that they had just made their first blunder on the handling of the murders. If Helen was indeed involved with Horace's death she would surely contact him advising him that they were to see him the next morning.

Bob said, "Possibly, and I did think of that, but like you, I am convinced that she is not involved and that her so-called friend is our man. There still is a tap on Mrs. Hastings phone isn't there?"

"Yes, and if by chance there is a call, we will know immediately."

FIFTEEN

WHEN THEY ARRIVED at Larry Adams Auto Shop, the next morning, Larry had not arrived. The shop was still closed. It was only seven in the morning so they decided to go have coffee and a donut at the Dunkin Donut shop directly across the street from the garage and wait for Larry to arrive.

When they sat down in the coffee shop, a man sitting at the window arose and approached agents Carle and Spedden and asked them, "I saw you two guys stop and found the Adams Auto Repair Shop closed. Are you waiting to see Larry? Does that son of a bitch owe you money too?"

Agent Carle replied," Yes we stopped at the shop looking for Mr. Adams, but no, he does not owe us any money. We just wanted to discuss business with him."

"Well, your mighty lucky, that son of a bitch who

runs that shop owes me over fifty five hundred dollars for parts, and he has been putting me off for three months. He's going to pay me or I'm going to have his shop closed up until he does."

"How can you make him close up?"

"Because I have three of his bad checks, and the county sheriff will close him up for issuing bad checks and not paying me as he was directed to do by the Judge of the court. They will haul his ass to jail."

"Has he been in court for issuing bad checks?

"You bet he has, I'm just one of a dozen who supplied him with tools or auto parts. There he is now, I have to go the bastard just went in his shop. I don't want him to run off before I see him today."

Agents Carle and Spedden, decided to wait in Dunkin Donuts, until that man left the shop.

"Boy, I think our hunch on this guy is right. I'll bet he is after Mrs. Hastings's money for sure just as we discussed on the way down here."

"It sure looks like it Bill. After we interview him, I think we should make some local inquires on him while we are in Salisbury. Didn't Mrs. Hastings mention that he was a county commissioner? We might just start there. Let's go sit in the car in case he comes out and tries to leave."

Their wait in the car was interrupted by two almost simultaneous loud bangs. Agent Carle yelled, "Oh my God, those were gun shots; let's get over there quick

I'll take the front of the building you call the police and take the back of the building."

The call was made and the police arrived shortly after the overhead door suddenly went down. The agents then presented their badges to the police and with their guns in their hands they knocked on the door. There was no response.

Agent Spedden ran to the back of the building and announced "FBI, open the door and come out with your hands over your head." There was still no response.

Three additional police cars and six more policemen arrived and a tear gas cartridge was fired into the building through a glass window. Shortly a voice was heard, "Don't shoot, I'm coming out. I have been hit. Please call an ambulance."

"Mr. Adams has been shot too and he has a gun. I shot that bastard in the chest. He tried to kill me. I hit him with a shot. He still has a gun, and is still lying in his office on the floor. I'm afraid to move. He wants to kill me."

Two ambulances arrived in a few minutes and the police opened the rear door, entered the building carefully, and found and handcuffed the man near the door crouched behind a stack of automobile tires, carried him out of the building and placed him under guard in one of the two ambulances and it left with him for the Peninsula General hospital.

On the way to the hospital he was asked why he closed the overhead doors. He replied, "Mr. Adams was wounded and still had a gun, I didn't want him to get away. I was able to crawl near the door and wounded. My gun was still on the floor in Mr. Adam's office."

"Mr. Adams, we have the man that shot you and we are coming in to see that you get to the hospital, don't shoot."

"Thank God you arrived when you did, that guy was trying to rob me and he shot me in the shoulder before I pulled my gun out of the desk drawer."

"Ok, don't worry, we have him in custody. We are coming in; but you must put that gun down and your hands in the air".

"Ok, don't shoot, I'm hit in the shoulder and I can't get up, I need to go to the hospital."

"An ambulance is already here and waiting for you -- careful now, we are coming in your office to get you now. Throw your gun toward the open door so we can see it."

After Larry Adams was loaded in the ambulance along with two police officers, Agents Spedden and Carle, described in detail what transpired just prior to the shooting.

They advised the police detective the shop owner, Mr. Adams was under investigation as a suspect in the murder of a man up in Delaware, and repeated the story told to them by the other man whose name they did not know. It was given to them by one of the Salisbury police officers as Garrett Cooper who owned an auto parts store in Salisbury.

"We would like to have his gun and if possible the slug that shot Mr. Cooper if you will release it to us."

"Our office will have it returned to you for use in our prosecution of this case and we are requesting that Larry Adams not be released from custody until our office here in Salisbury completes a request for his transfer to Delaware to face our murder charges should the slugs match with that found in our victim."

All was agreed to.

The Salisbury times headline the next morning read; ***Local Business man is a suspect in the Seaford Reunion murders.*** The Wilmington Mornings news carried a similar story.

The FBI, made a thorough investigation of both men involved in the Maryland shooting and it was reported that Mr. Adams had previously been warned about carrying a concealed gun when he was attempting to collect a bill that was owed to him.

He also had been arrested two times with a DUI charge. They were told that he was found to be heavily in debt and was near a foreclosure on his property and business by the bank. He had been sued for cheating a woman in Berlin, Maryland out of $5,000 she had given him to take to the bank for her. He repaid the funds and she dropped the charges.

After he was treated for his wound while under guard at the hospital, he was released to the FBI who took him in custody as a suspect in the murder of Horace Hastings and he was confined in the State prison in Georgetown, Delaware.

Garrett Cooper, who shot Larry Adams was released on his own recognition; but, was to face a trial in Wicomico County, Maryland for carrying an unlicensed and concealed weapon and threatening Mr. Adams. Then after a stern lecture from the Maryland judge, advising him that he should stop trying to take the law in his own hands was released.

When the FBI tests on the bullets removed from Horace and Garrett Cooper confirmed that they were both fired from the same gun. Agent Carle took it on himself to contact Helen Hastings.

"Helen, I am indeed sorry that all of this has happened to you, but I am certain that your life with Larry Adams would have been nothing but more trouble."

"Bill, I had no intention of any kind of life with Larry. I am very upset that I was given such a glowing recommendation on him by a close friend no less."

"Helen I'm really very sorry about Horace, but I'm very pleased that we have solved the mystery surrounding his death and have put Larry where he belongs. There is no question that he will be found guilty."

"I hate to even think about what he would have done had he got away with the murder. Our investigation on his character, indicated that he is very deep in debt, and had already cheated a lady in Berlin, Maryland out of several thousand dollars. We also found out that he had lied to you when he said he was a county commissioner."

"Yes, Bill I found that out myself yesterday when I called their office in Salisbury and they told me that he was not a member of the commission and that they did not know who he was."

"I tried to call you and let you know but you were reported out of town. I suppose you may have been in Salisbury when I called them."

"If you will recall, Bill I told you that I had absolutely no interest in Larry, I'm afraid I let him talk me into something I should have known better to do. So his arrest only makes me want to thank you."

"After your visit with me the other day, I began thinking that perhaps Larry wasn't everything I was led to believe. I got concerned when you were asking me about Horace's life insurance policy. I made up my mind to drop him completely. Mr. Faulkner has been engaged to settle my estate. Of course the divorce case will be closed completely."

"I want to thank you for not letting me make a bad mistake. All I want now is to get on with my life, get it all back in order, and in good graces with Horace's family."

"Bill tell me the truth, did you think that I really had anything to do with Horace's death? After my interview yesterday, I couldn't sleep for thinking that not only had I lost Horace but that I had lost you too."

"You have not lost me Helen, I want to renew what we had going for us at the university. I never questioned your innocence, but I did have to do my job. I do love you Helen."

"I love you to Bill, you told me once that you were never to tell anyone anything that was not common knowledge."

"Yes, I did say that didn't I. I guess I will have to make it common knowledge somehow. How about having dinner with me tonight at the Flagship where all your friends go, so we can make some plans on our future relationship and really get the gossip rolling?"

"Yes I would love that Bill. Do you think that Larry could have killed Jeanne and Harriet too?"

"At this point, I have to say no. We have no information or reason to believe that he had any reason for doing that. It is our belief now that Larry assumed that his murder of Horace would be covered up and assumed to have been done by the same person that killed the girls. Helen, please don't tell anyone about what I just said. That's only my personal opinion."

"Why would you not want that to be known?"

"Because as long as they think that the killer is in jail, people will possibly tell us things that they were afraid to talk to us about before."

"Bill, I know that you have a lot of problems to be worked out and I am so happy you have solved the case on Horace's murder. To celebrate our finding Horace's murderer, I wonder if you would consider having dinner with me somewhere out of town instead of the Flagship. Perhaps we could find a nice restaurant in Ocean City. I want to get away from all of this for a time and celebrate. Maybe even have a few manhattans like the old days."

"I would certainly enjoy that Helen, Ocean City it will be and I promise no more questions. I do want to have a good meal with a young and attractive lady for a change. I get tired of looking at Bob Spedden's face across the table two times a day."

"To be honest Helen, I am hoping that we can pick up our relationship right where we stopped at the university when I moved to Tennessee. I confess that I am truly hurt that such a thing could happen to you and I want to see you out enjoying life again."

"Well how thoughtful of you Bill. Let me know what time would be convenient for you because I will have to find a babysitter. But Bill, you will have to remember that I have two children now and our relationship would have to include them."

"No baby sitter Helen; bring them along. I am sure they would enjoy a walk down the boardwalk."

"Helen, you have never asked me, but just for information, I am not married, was never divorced, and I have no financial problems, and you are free to check me out, and beside that I have no lady friend."

"There you go warning me again to watch who I date, you truly are all FBI. I would find it hard to believe that you have no lady friend. You were a ladies' man in college; at least you were until I roped you in until you left us for Tennessee and you wrote me that you were dating a girl there."

"I didn't say that I had never had a lady friend, I only wanted to tell you that I was available, should you be interested. But my job really does put a damper on any kind of commitments anymore."

"Great we now understand each other, do we still have a dinner date this evening, or not?"

"Yes Bill, the children and I would be happy to join you at dinner and you are wrong Mr. FBI, you do have a girlfriend. Me. About five is that Ok?"

"Yes, five it is. We will be eating in Ocean City at some great seafood place where Bob and I ate one night last week."

"What will Bob do for dinner?"

"Oh he has a business dinner date with one of your classmates who may have some information on Jeanne Records. He will be interviewing her hopefully to get some clues on the other murders."

"Is that why you are asking me to dinner?"

"No way; I promised you no questions remember?"

"Yes, but I know that you are still FBI, and that you still have two other murders to solve."

SIXTEEN

THE TEAM WAS jubilant that the question they had, as to why Horace was killed, had finally been solved. Their focus now could be directed back to the two ladies, and rape was now the most probable motive.

Douglas Weaver was removed from the list of suspects. His fight with Horace was no longer a reason to hold him as a suspect in Horace's murder and they had nothing that let them believe that he murdered or raped the girls.

Larry Adams, the friend of Horace's wife, was now behind bars and charged with Horace's murder in the first degree. He stated that he had hopes of becoming either Helen's husband or her financial manager. He admitted that he had pocketed the money she gave him and he had not paid for a title search nor had he hired a private investigator.

The insurance company paid Helen's claim of one and

a half million dollars, and the funds were immediately deposited in a trust account, with Helen as the Trustee.

Helen called Horace's two brothers and his parents and asked them to meet at her house at 3:00 so she could advise them of her intentions regarding the poultry business and the farm operations.

On their arrival she introduced her attorney Henry Faulkner and then she announced it was her plan to stay on the farm so her children could grow up close to their grandparents, but that she had decided that she would start looking for a teaching job working with children with learning problems, for which she had been trained at the university.

She added that if that job required her relocation, she would hope that the brothers would guide and assist Steve in running the farm lands for her until she decided what she would do if that became necessary.

She told them that Mr. Faulkner was going to serve as her property manager, and handle the rental of her six rental properties in the cities of Seaford and in Laurel, and that she had asked him to prepare papers on the disposal of the chicken and farm operations, and that she was certain that he would have the paperwork for them soon.

"I promise you that there will be no action taken on the disposal of anything until I meet with you all in a week or so when Mr. Faulkner completes the paperwork. No questions please, there has been nothing decided or set in stone at the moment. You will have an opportunity to make suggestions at that time."

The brothers both thanked her for saying that she would not take any steps to break up the business or farm without discussing it with them because they were working on a proposal themselves.

Then in closing, Mr. Faulkner announced that he would have Helen's plan for the disposal of the farm and poultry business ready in a few day and he would ask for another meeting at that time.

He closed the meeting with an announcement he had been instructed to pay out of Helen's personal account the sum of fifty thousand dollars to Horace's church in Horace's memory and again Horace's mother embraced Helen and thanked her.

Chief Daley in the regular morning meeting of the agents and the city police team asked them to prepare a report for the states Attorney General that would be made available to him for use in the prosecution of Larry Adams for the murder of Horace Hastings.

They were then told they needed to focus back on the rape and murder of the two women Harriet O'Brien and Jeanne Records.

Agent Carle briefed them in the morning on all the reports, accusations, etc. that had been confirmed or suggestions to date.

"Rape is the current most likely motive for the death of Jeanne Records; but the reason for Harriet's murder is still undetermined, but rape is not yet off the table in the death of Harriet ether."

"It is the opinion of several of our team members that the rapist was not an outsider, but one that was well known by Jeanne and Harriet."

Agent Carle stated, "Homer Price is still the prime suspect on Jeanne's murder because of an accusation in the past that he had raped a girl of the class, who refused to press charges against him."

"We have nothing to prove his guilt or that will convince a jury that he was the rapist and killer of either woman. We have to solidify that accusation."

"The DNA reports have still not been received and we will just have to wait for that report to determine his innocence or guilt."

"But we need to strengthen our case against him assuming, that the DNA will find him as the actual rapist based on the DNA samples taken. Even then, we will have to prove the sex act was not consensual with Harriet because the Coroner claims that she was not raped."

"She was pregnant but he could not confirm she had been raped and he further stated that the DNA of the semen found in her body may or may not match the DNA semen found in Jeanne Records who definitely had been raped. The DNA would solve that question."

"We also still have Alfred Warrington as a possible suspect for the murder of Harriet O'Brien, and we don't want to overlook Robert Miller. He is still missing and unaccounted for. There was a mention in an earlier interview that Mr. Miller was at the Flagship Restaurant the night that Horace and Douglas had their encounter in the parking lot. We are rather sure he was the man Harriet had dinner with that night. "

"We need to dig into Robert Miller. Let's find our just where he is. Who did he talk to when he was known to be in Seaford, other than that golfing guy who called us?"

"There are many, including myself that are concerned that he may have been killed, and his body has just not been found. There are others that suspect he may be the murderer we are really looking for."

"Did he rape the two women, kill them, and then just take off until all of this quiets down? Bob Spedden and I will be going to Jimmy's restaurant early tomorrow morning so that we can talk to some of the locals and determine if we can find what the people of Seaford are saying and to see if we can get a lead on where Mr. Miller may be located."

"We feel that he just may have told someone where he was going. He surely talked with someone in Seaford other than Harriet and that golfer. Hopefully we can find someone else that he talked with."

"The rest of you can start scanning the stacks of reports we have created from our interviews and perhaps you may just find something. Who else may have talked with Harriet even a week or so ahead of her being found murdered."

"Check on the same things for Jeanne Records. I feel that she may have been killed for what she may have known about Harriet's death. Remember she was not murdered and raped for several days after Harriet was found. Who did Jeanne talk to at the reunion or around that time? Let's get busy and wrap up this investigation."

Agents Carle and Spedden arrived at Jimmy's restaurant shortly after it opened. They told Jimmy that they would be talking with his customers and asked if he had any objection their doing that in his restaurant.

Jimmy stated that there would be no problem with that and if they were willing he would personally ask a question now and then just to get the gang, as he called them, talking.

Agent Carle told him that would certainly be helpful in accomplishing what they were attempting to do.

As usual, by 8:20 am the restaurant had three tables of up to six of the so-called gang drinking their coffee and talking about everything imaginable, but mostly about Horace's murder and his murderer, the political topics of the day, women, or telling sexy jokes.

The restaurant owner Jimmy Johnson, approached the tables refilling the gang's cups, and said, "Mr. Carle, what's going on with the rape cases, anything new happening? I'm sure glad that you got Horace's killer. Do you think he was the man who raped and killed Harriet and Jeanne?"

"Well Jimmy, we have not dismissed that possibility yet, but we have to make certain that we can prove who did them. In the mean time we are busy tracking down some leads we already have and we are hoping we can wrap it all up soon."

"Right now we are looking for another classmate who we have been unable to locate. We are anxious to talk with anyone who talked with him when he was here in Seaford just before the reunion. His name is Robert Miller. By chance, do any of you men know him and can anyone of you tell us if he came in here for breakfast or dinner when he was in Seaford?"

Jimmy himself replied, "Oh yes, I saw him here. He came in several days for breakfast. Ray Nichols introduced me to him and asked if I remembered him. At first I didn't recognize him although I knew he looked familiar."

"When he was in school he was a thin boy; but in the five years since I last saw him, he sure filled out and I told him that."

"He said that he was working out at the gym, most every day for about thirty minutes. That's about all I remember of his visits here, but he was busy talking with all of us in here."

Ben Beiser, sitting at a nearby table interrupted, "I saw Robert when he was in here. He was sitting with Ray Nichols, Fred Hedges and I one day, but I can't remember just what day that was."

"Robert told us that he was trying to find an old acquaintance in Virginia and I remember him asking us if we knew just where the city of Jarrett was located in Virginia."

"I didn't know. I had never heard of that town. I offered to go see if I had a Virginia map in the car, but Fred Adkins told him it was located right on Interstate 95 south of Richmond, and that a Seaford girl that he knew married a guy from Jarrett named Haskell or something like that."

"What was the name of the Seaford girl that he knew?"

"I don't know. You will have to ask Fred."

"Mr. Carle they may still live down there. Fred told Robert her name but I don't remember what it was either, and Fred told him she could probably help him find who he was looking for once he got down there if she still lived there."

"Did he say how he found out that the person he was looking for lived in Jarrett?"

"Yes as a matter of fact he did. He said that Harriet had told him when they were having dinner the previous night. Robert said that Harriet told him she had written to her several time after she left Seaford, and at that time she lived in a little town named Jarrett."

"Good lord, I hope that isn't why Harriet was raped and murdered. Do you think that Robert could have raped Harriet and then killed her?"

"There is that possibility, he is still missing. But we are not certain that Harriet had in fact been raped. Did Mr. Miller tell you who he was trying to locate; or if it was a man or woman? You just said Harriet had written to her several times. If that is true then he must be looking for a girl."

"Robert never mention who he was looking for all he

said was that he was looking for an old acquaintance. But yes he did say what Harriet said about writing."

Just as Ben had finished telling of the conversation with Robert Miller, Ray Nichols came in and sat at the table.

"Here's Ray, coming in now Mr. Carle, maybe he can add something that I forgot. Ray, I was telling Mr. Carle, about what Robert Miller told us here in Jimmy's about looking for someone he knew some time ago. Remember that conversation?"

"Jimmy, I'll have coffee, biscuits, and eggs over light with sausage paddies, I'm in a hurry. Yes, I remember sitting with him. He was looking for someone in Virginia as I recall, and wanted to know if we knew where that town was. I never heard of it but someone told him where it was. Is that right?"

"Yep, that's right. Fred Adkins told him where Jarrett was."

Agent Carle asked, "Can you recall anything else that was said over that breakfast?"

"Let me think, oh yes, I think that he said he was going to look her up while he was in Virginia."

"Are you sure he said her. Was it a lady he was going to see?"

"Yes, I am sure of that, he told me that outside as he was about to drive off. He said something about her being divorced and she just might be interested in renewing an old friendship. He was sure excited I know that."

Ray Nichols interrupted, "Well the only relationship,

I ever remember Robert as having was with the girl that works in the library. Yes, Kathy Black but it couldn't have been her because she lives right here in Seaford."

"Come to think of it Ben, didn't Kathy quit school and marry some guy and move away? I think Robert was dating Kathy and she just quit dating him and ran off with some other guy."

"Yes, that's right Kathy was the love of his life. Do you imagine that he didn't know that Kathy was back here in Seaford? If so, he's going to be surprised when he finds out she was right here in Seaford, and that she has a little boy to boot."

"Yes, I bet that is the answer because Jeanne Records told me that Harriet had mentioned to her that Robert had asked her if she knew where Kathy went when she left Seaford before graduation. Harriet told him that she had eloped and moved to Virginia to live."

"That's just like Harriet; she may have just answered his question, without realizing that Robert didn't know Kathy was back in Seaford or perhaps she just forgot that Kathy was back in Seaford."

"If that's the case, old Bob will be running all over Virginia looking for her. He'll probably be back here soon or just go on back to Wilmington where he lives. I bet he's in Wilmington."

"Gentlemen, I have to run, but thanks again for talking with me. I am sure that you are as anxious as we are to bring this matter to a close. When we get all the data together perhaps we will have the guilty person behind bars."

When agent Carle got back to the station he placed a call to Fred Adkins and was told that the girl he knew who moved to Jarrett was named Esther Hitchens. He did not remember her married name.

He then placed a call to the Richmond FBI branch office and asked them to inquire at the Jarrett post office, the Chamber of Commerce, for the address of a lady who lived in Jarrett named Esther Hitchens, and that might not be her married name, if they could sort all that out, could they try to find anyone who knew of a girl that had moved there a a few years back named Kathy Black, and she too may have been using a married name.

About mid afternoon the next day, agent Carle was told by the FBI office in Richmond that Robert Miller had been in Jarrett looking for a lady named Kathy Black and after some questioning, they were directed to the only family name Black, in the area, and this turned out to be the right family. It was Kathy's grandfather. Grover Black,

The agent was told that Kathy's grandmother had just died about two years ago, and Kathy had moved back to Seaford, Delaware shortly after that. Her grandfather told the agent that Kathy had never married and that Mr. Robert Miller may have been the father of her child.

He told the agent that he had refused to give Mr. Miller any information about Kathy because it was the wish of his wife, his daughter, and his granddaughter

Kathy not to tell anyone that Kathy had never married or to tell Mr. Miller where Kathy was, should he ever contact him.

Mr. Black lied to Mr. Miller because he knew Kathy would not want him to know where she was. He told Mr. Miller that she lived somewhere in Richmond and that he didn't know her address or any telephone number.

The report also indicated that Mr. Miller had checked out of the Jarrett Motel later the morning after talking to Mr. Black. His make of car and license plate as found on his registration was listed as a Lexus van with a Delaware vanity tag RMILLER.

The agents determined that if he was heading back to Seaford or Wilmington Delaware he would be back in Delaware by this time, unless he decided to spend a few days looking for her in Richmond, but an alert was put out in New Castle, Kent, and Sussex counties in Delaware anyway.

Four days later Robert was finally located at the same motel in Seaford, Delaware where he had been staying earlier, and he was picked up for questioning as a suspect in the murders of both Harriet O'Brien and Jeanne Records. At the police station in Seaford, agents Carle and Spedden read him his rights and proceeded to interview him.

"Mr. Miller we have missing person reports on you that was issued by both your mother and your business partner in Wilmington."

Interrupting Mr. Carle, he said, "I talked with both of them just this morning, and I told them that I would be home the day after tomorrow. I have a business appointment with a gentleman here in Seaford tomorrow morning. I have been in Virginia seeking information, and was also preparing a presentation I was to give him at the meeting tomorrow. "

"Well they have not told anyone that you had been heard from; but that is not why we are questioning you just now. You are a suspect in the murder of Harriet O'Brien."

"What? You mean that she was murdered? I just saw her a week or so ago. In fact, I had dinner with Harriet at the Flagship Restaurant the night before I left for Virginia. I surely did not rape or kill either of them. Who said I did such a thing?"

"You said you had dinner with Miss O'Brien, what was the purpose of your having dinner with her? Were you a close friend of hers?"

"Not really, I was just asking Harriet where an old friend of mine went when she left Seaford five years ago. She told me where she went in Virginia. It was a small town named Jarrett. I could not locate her in Jarrett but was told by her grandfather that she went to Richmond and that is the area where I have been for the past week. I was looking for her in the day time and working on my presentation at nights."

"Yes we are aware of that, but you were likely the last person that we know about to see Harriet alive. That is the only reason we brought you in here."

"Well I wasn't the last person to see her either, because

just as we were about to leave the restaurant a guy about my age, approached our table. She evidently knew him well because she introduced me to him and told me that he was a good friend."

"I was standing up and preparing to leave. Harriet and I had met each other at the restaurant. I thanked her for having dinner with me and answering some questions that I had for her. I told her that I would see her again before I went back to Wilmington. The guy sat down and started talking to Harriet just as I left."

"Yes, we are aware of that too. Was his name by chance, Homer?"

"No, I know Homer Price if that is the man you are asking about. It definitely wasn't him. The man was about my age, but I don't honestly remember his name."

"You said that Harriet introduced him to you, How about George?"

"No not a George. I'm sorry I just can't remember his name. I'm sure he was not one of our classmates though."

"How about the name Albert, does that ring a bell?"

"Yes that's it; his name was Albert, no that's not right; it was Alfred, his name was Alfred. I did not know him. I don't think he graduated with us."

"How does Alfred Warrington sound to you?"

"Yes, that's it. Alfred Warrington was his name and Harriet said he was a friend. She told him that I was about to leave and she asked if he would like to join her in a drink. He turned to me and asked, if that was Ok. I told him I was just leaving. So l was not the last person to see Harriet, Alfred was with her after I left the restaurant."

"Then just as I left the restaurant. I saw Jeanne Records coming in the restaurant with a man who I did not know. She recognized me because she called me by my name Robert."

"She didn't introduce the man she was with; but I didn't stop to talk to her either. I didn't recognize him at all. I was in a hurry because I wanted to get prepared for my trip to Virginia. I had the information I was looking for."

"Mr. Miller, can you describe the man that was with Jeanne when you were leaving the restaurant?"

"No, I can't, all that I can tell you about him is that I do remember that he was well dressed and that Jeanne never introduced me to him at all. I'm not sure if she forgot to do so, or if she thought I knew him, at any rate I was in a hurry to check the phone book in Virginia and I didn't ask her who he was either. I think I told her that I was in a hurry but I really can't remember if I did that or not."

"When I got back to my motel to call Virginia, I realized that I did not know the last name of the person I wanted to call and decided to drive down there in the morning."

"Mr. Miller, we are at the point now where I need some answers. Just exactly when did you leave to go to Virginia?"

"I was excited and pleased about some news that

Harriet had given me and I left the next morning after having breakfast at Jimmy's. That would have been on June 20th two days before the reunion."

"I even forgot that I had a date to play golf on the 21st with a guy I met at the du Pont Country Club until I was on Interstate 95 in Maryland heading for Virginia. I would have called him to cancel our game had I remembered."

"Where did you spend the night?

"I stopped in Richmond about two or three o'clock in the afternoon. I was getting tired and I wanted to get to Jarrett, where I was heading, early in the morning so I could have all day to locate someone there. It was at a Days Inn on the north side of Richmond. I have my receipt if you need that."

"Yes, that will help us to place you out of Seaford when one of the girls was murdered. Bob it may help us, if you could tell us just what Harriet told you that you were so pleased about."

"Mr. Carle that is a very long story, when I was in high school I was very close to a girl named Kathy Black. We were very close friends. We were planning on getting married as soon as we graduated in late May of our senior year."

"Then just before Christmas I called Kathy and asked if she wanted to go to a movie and she told me that she didn't want to go because she was not feeling well."

"I called her several times after that and she told me that she didn't want me to call her anymore. I asked her why and she simply told me that things had changed."

"I was really upset and was wondering if she had found another boy, but I couldn't find any reason for her actions and just decided that she was getting cold feet about our plans on getting married after we graduated. The next thing I heard was that she had quit school got married and moved out of town."

"Needless to say I was really down in the dumps. I had never dated another girl in school and I just wanted to get out of Seaford. I even convinced my mother to move to Wilmington with me after I graduated and had accepted a job in Wilmington."

"I convinced my mother that I could make more money in Wilmington; but the truth of the matter was, I just wanted to get away from Seaford and every one that knew about Kathy and me."

"I quit going to all school activities and could hardly wait for my graduation. I was truly broken hearted. I left Seaford the day after I graduated to find work."

"Then when I got the note about our first class reunion, I decided that perhaps, I should go just to see how they were all doing and I would be there on business anyway. I had not seen any of my classmates since I graduated, and I had become rather successful in business and I guess I just wanted to let them know that I had done Ok."

"I have never dated another girl since that time and to be honest, I was anxious to see if any of them could tell me what ever happened to Kathy. I ran into Harriet at a Deli parking lot and talked with her for several minutes. She was in a hurry but agreed to meet me at the Flagship

Restaurant that next evening and would bring me up to date on everyone."

"I have already told you about when I met Harriet at the Flagship Restaurant. But to continue we had dinner and talked about all of our classmates, and eventually I asked her about Kathy."

"She told me that Kathy had quit school because she got married to some boy from Virginia and moved down there but that the marriage had failed and she was now divorced. When she told me that Kathy was divorced, I couldn't help but wonder if there was a chance that Kathy and I could get together again. I think I am still in love with her."

"I asked Harriet if she knew where Kathy went to in Virginia and she told me that it was to a small town in Virginia named Jarrett, adding that she had stayed in touch with her for about two years while she was there."

"About that time, her friend approached our booth, and that was the end of our conversation. I had already found out what I wanted and had made up my mind that I was going down to that small town in Virginia and see if I could find her. I was hoping that there was a possibility that we could get together again."

"Then you didn't know that she had moved back to Seaford?"

"Seaford, you have to be kidding, No, I finally got the postmaster in Jarrett to tell me her grandfather's name, and he told me that she was living in Richmond. He didn't know the address. After searching the entire phone book of families name Black, in Richmond, I just gave up and decided to come back to Seaford, to finish the business I had pending there, and head back to Wilmington. And here I am."

"If that friend of Harriet's had not showed up just when he did, Harriet would probably have mentioned that Kathy was back in Seaford."

"Bob, we have confirmed your times in Virginia and I'm pleased to tell you that you are free to go. I would suggest that you go to the library and see Kathy. I do hope that the two of you can get together again."

"Yes, I plan to see her as soon as I can. Thanks for the kind words."

SEVENTEEN

ROBERT WENT TO his hotel and took a shower and then called the library and asked for Kathy. "Kathy, this is Bob Miller. I am here in Seaford and I wonder if we could get together for a few minutes to talk? It has been a long time."

"Bob is this really you? I was told that you were missing."

"Yes, I guess I was by some people. I was in Virginia trying to find you. It's a long story. I will tell you all about what actually happened if you will just give me a few minutes to talk with you. What time do you get off work? I do want to see you before I go back to Wilmington. I was hoping that we could get together for dinner tonight. I was told that you are divorced. Is that really true?"

"Bob, I have a son. Norman. He is four years old and yes I am not married. I will tell you all about that too."

"I would be happy to have dinner with you this evening; but first I will have to see if my baby sitter is free. But better still, why don't you just come to my house, and I will prepare something special for us. I would really prefer that because I have so much to tell you and I would not feel as free to talk to you as I would be here at home. I get off work at 4:00 and if you could make it to my house. Let's say around 6:00; that will allow me time to pick up Norm from Day Care, stop by the food market for a few items, and prepare the meal."

"No Kathy, I don't want you to go to all that trouble. We can take him with us. I would like to see him anyway. What restaurant would you prefer to go to? I was thinking about going down to Salisbury to that Seafood restaurant located just off old US 13 on the north side of Highway 50 to Ocean City that you and I used to go to on most Saturday nights. How does that sound?"

"Oh Bob, that would be great. I haven't been there since I last went there with you. I don't know if they are still in business or not."

"Yes, they are still there and the food is still great as ever. It has changed owners but it all looks just the same. I was told that a man from Laurel bought the business. I had dinner there a week or so before I went to Virginia looking for you. I have forgot its' new name. I will pick you and little Norman up about seven o'clock. But I will need to know where your home is."

"Oh yes, of course. I bought a house in the new development just in back of the Seaford Shopping Center.

Look for the sign on the left that reads Ayers Acres. I live on the second street on the right and in the third house on the left. It is number 1205 Jasmine Avenue and that number is on my mailbox."

Bob found the house with no problem and knocked on the door at just a few minutes after 6:00 pm. Kathy opened the door, took Bob's hand and asked him to come in. Little Norman, ran to him and said, "Are you the man taking us to out to eat? I want a burger and fries, and a shake."

"Yes, I'm the man; I like burgers and shakes too."

"Bob, would it be OK with you to wait awhile before we leave. I have a lot to tell you that should have been said years ago?"

"Surely, I have a lot to tell you also."

"I am not certain just how much you know about what happened to me when we were back in high school and I regret now the decisions I made at that time."

"I made the decision that I took, because I didn't want you to know what really happened because of my love for you. You were ill one night when I went to the school to watch the basketball games."

"Norm, go get your red fire truck you just got last week to show to Mr. Miller."

"A boy offered to take me home after the game was over and against my wish he drove me to The Island and raped me. I was depressed and embarrassed beyond explanation over the incident and I didn't want you to know about it. I knew that you would have done something drastic."

"You can bet on that, who was the boy?"

"Later Bob, please let me finish, I decided that I would try to keep the rape quiet, not only because I was embarrassed but because, I had kept my virginity just for you as you well know."

Bob took Kathy in his arms. And they kissed.

"How many times did we come close only to quit because we wanted to wait until we were married? I was afraid that if it became known that I had been raped, you would not want to marry a girl that everyone knew had been raped."

"Then at the end of my month, I found out that I was pregnant by that rape."

"I was lost as what to do. I talked to my mother and grandmother about what to do. I told them that I would not have an abortion. I think that is a sin against God."

Norm returned to show Bob the toy fire engine, and then started playing with it on the floor.

"After many dreadful days, my grandmother, suggested that I come down to her house in Virginia and that we could start a rumor in Seaford, with my mother telling everyone that I had eloped and been married."

"Norm, I bet Mr. Miller would like to see that other truck – the yellow one."

"Well it worked and no one ever knew about what happened except I did tell about the rape to Elizabeth Truitt, who later married John Bennett, when she asked me what had happened between you and I."

"Later the police contacted me about the rape and I

denied the rape or to press any charges. I just wanted to forget it and live with it. Elizabeth promised me that she would never reveal the truth and even helped me to spread the rumor of my being married."

"Everything fell in place. I went to Virginia to live with my grandmother until Norman was born and Elizabeth told me that the classmates were under the impression that I had indeed eloped."

"She told me later that you had left Seaford but she didn't know where. She told me many times that I owed it to you to tell you what had really happed. I wish now that I had taken her advice."

"I decided to let you know what really happened, but I did not know how to contact you. I was going to ask you what I should do short of admitting the rape."

"Kathy, I sure wish that you had, I was devastated when I heard you had gone off and married someone else. I don't honestly know what I would have done if I had known about the situation at that time; but I do know that its history now and it has no impact on how I feel about you."

"My only hope now is that we can put all of this behind us and that we can get together again. I have never forgotten the relationship we once had."

"I have not forgotten those days either Bob. I do still love you."

"I still have the engagement ring that I bought that I was going to offer you on Christmas Eve of that year. If I had it with me now, I would offer it to you right now."

"I would certainly accept it. What about Norman Bob, could you handle that?"

"That will never be a problem for me. I always dreamed of having a son. I still love you and have never lost that love. Will you really marry me Kathy? I can promise you and little Norman that I will protect you and care for you both as long as I live."

"Yes, Bob, I will marry you. Will we live in Seaford or Wilmington?"

"I hope that you will agree to go to Wilmington. I have a very successful business there and I think that it would be best that we leave the past bad memories down here in Seaford."

"In Wilmington we can start living our own lives. We can apply for a change in Norman's last name and I can adopt him. Yes, Norman Miller; that's a good name. Perhaps he can become as successful as the writer Norman Miller. Kathy, I want you to know that since you left Seaford, I have never dated or been with another woman."

"I have never dated again either Bob and honestly I have never had the desire to do so. Remember we had decided when we were in our senior year that we would wait until we got married, and how close we came several times, well I'm still waiting but you can spend this night with me; if you wish. I'm willing to break that promise. I do still love you."

"Kathy as much as I would love to make love to you tonight; or at this very moment let's not forget the promise we made to each other back then. Let's wait until we get married."

"Oh thank you Bob."

They kissed and held each other close for several minutes. Little Norman said, "I want to go eat. I want a burger and some fries."

Kathy and Bob laughed and Bob whispered, "Well your virginity is saved by the call of hunger."

Kathy whispered, "Bob, I am no longer a virgin."

"You are in my eyes Kathy, let's get going before you are not or Norm starves to death."

"Bob when can we get married?

"Is tonight too soon? Just kidding, we can go see the minister tomorrow, set a date, and make arrangements for your move to Wilmington. I want you to meet my mother again."

"She still talks about you all the time and has never quite figured out what happened between us. What do you think about getting married in Wilmington in a week or so? If that is where you want to live?"

"If it is alright with you, I would prefer having my minister marry us here in Seaford, and then go to Wilmington. He has been so helpful to me since before I left Seaford and after I came back. I never told him about the rape. He thinks that I just eloped and got into a bad marriage."

"I just wish my mother could have lived just a little longer. She tried her best to talk me into contacting you. I sure wish now that I had listened to her."

"I wish that you had too. If you had told me what happened, it would not have changed my mind about marrying you after we graduated, but I would probably have suggested back then that we should have been married right away."

"Then Seaford it will be. Let's go talk to him in the morning to make all the arrangements. If it is Ok with you, I would like for the FBI agent William Carle, to be my best man. I really don't know too many people in Seaford anymore. He was instrumental in getting us back together again and I will be forever grateful to him."

"That would be OK with me. I will call Betty Bennett to be my maid of honor. She is my very best friend and I know that she will be delighted that we have gotten back together again. . She kept my secret all these years. She is pregnant and due very soon. I will have to see if she could do that."

"Where would we live in Wilmington?

"That will be your choice, I would prefer to live outside the city closer to Newark to be closer to my office in Stanton, but we will take a look at the many developments and I will let you make the decision. My mother and I live on Arundel Drive in Stanton just north of the Kirkwood highway."

"Can I go to Wilmton too? But let's go eat first, I'm hungry. You two can talk while I eat my burger, and fries. And I want a chocolate shake. Are you going to be my daddy?"

"Yes Norm, I'm going to be your daddy and you can order anything on the menu tonight, how about that?"

"Yeah, then can I have a peach pie with ice cream too? I can't wait to tell Freddie that I'm going to get a new daddy. He got a new one too."

When they returned to Kathy's house after dinner and after Kathy had put Norman to bed, they watched a movie "*The Eleanor and Lou Gehrig Story*" on the TV and sat together cuddled up like teenagers and after the show was over Bob told Kathy that he had better leave.

Kathy told him, "Bob, I know that we just promised each other again that we would wait until we got married, but I don't want you to leave. Won't you stay here with me? I think we have waited long enough."

Bob put his arms around Kathy and told her, "I think we have waited long enough too."

The next morning, they made an appointment with Kathy's minister and set a date for the marriage to be performed following the regular Sunday worship service two weeks later.

Kathy made arrangements with the church's women's organization to cater a reception for the entire church membership in the new Fellowship Hall of her church following the service and then the wedding.

Bill Carle and Betty Bennett were called about being their best man and bride's maid and the date was confirmed. Betty said that she could handle the task, if it was done within the next few weeks, as long as Kathy did not mind her grotesque stature such as it was.

Kathy said, "I love you Betty, and I want you standing beside me. I hope to look just like you soon."

They also asked Helen Hastings if her daughter would join Kathy's son who would be serving as a ring bearer, to be flower girl.

All was ready a little over five years after their original planned marriage.

EIGHTEEN

WHEN BOB CALLED Bill Carle and asked him if he would be his best man at his wedding, Bill told him that he would be very happy to have that honor, and the date, place, and time, were all setup.

Then Carle asked Bob, "Helen Hastings, and her two children, and I are having dinner tonight at Monaco's restaurant on Front Street, why don't you and Kathy have dinner with us and bring her little boy. I have never met him? I promise no questions on the past. I told Helen about you and Kathy and she told me that she was anxious to see you again."

"That sounds like a good idea. If Kathy agrees and I know she will. We will meet you there. What time?"

"Let's do it about 7:30 How's that?"

"OK, unless I call you, we will meet you there at 7:30. Love their spaghetti!"

Kathy agreed after Bob told her that Carle promised no more questions on her past. They arrived at the restaurant close to 7:30 and Bill, Helen, and her two children were already at a table set up for seven.

Helen was the first to talk, "Oh Bill, I forgot to tell you, I got a call from New Castle, Delaware this afternoon. My application to teach children with learning deficiencies has been approved. I will start teaching there this fall. I have to go up next week for a day of instruction. I'm so excited. I can finally put my training to use."

"That's wonderful Helen. I'm proud for you."

"Kathy I'm also happy that you and Bob are to be married."

"Yes Robert and I are back together again and this time we will be together for the rest of our lives. I was very sorry to learn about Horace. I hope that things work out for you and the children. What a terrible thing to happen to those two girls and to Horace. I just can't imagine who would have done such a thing."

"Yes Kathy, it was a terrible thing to happen, and to tell you the truth, I honestly thought that Horace may have had something to do with them; but now I don't think he did it. Horace and I were separated and I know he was messing with Harriet and I just think someone wanted him out of the way."

Agent Carle jumped into the conversation, "Hey, hey, we are supposed to be enjoying a good meal and an evening of friendship. No more talk on these cases tonight

Ok. Please remember any thoughts you may have on them and we will discuss them later."

"Yes, I will do that Bill, but I will tell you right now, that I know Horace was messing with Harriet. That was the start of our marital problems and I don't really care who knows it."

"I can understand why, we will discuss it later. I'm for spaghetti, how about you?"

"Yes, that sounds good to me."

Bob asked the waiter if he could get Norman a hamburger, some fries, and a chocolate milkshake off the lunch menu. The waiter said that could be arranged. Then he and Kathy both ordered spaghetti with meatballs and Bob ordered a bottle of wine.

Helen's two children ordered the same as Norman.

There was no more discussion on the reunion murders and Bob told Bill, "I am certainly pleased that you agreed to be my best man, when you have only met me this very week. But you got Kathy and I back together and I will be forever grateful for that."

The next morning Chief Daley called a meeting of the team and asked for an update.

Agent Carle told the chief that they had just received the DNA reports on Homer Price, Alfred Warrington, and Douglas Weaver, and the DNA semen tests on both Harriet and Jeanne.

"Guys, we have a serious problem here, the DNA on the semen samples of both women was identical, and that indicates that they both had sex or were raped by the same man, but, the problem we now face is that none of our suspects match with the DNA samples."

"I talked with the state's Attorney General, and he told me that he would not be able to prosecute either of them for the rape or murder of the two women."

"The Attorney General did state that he would try Homer Price on the rape of the two girls in high school even though it had been five years ago, if either of the girls would agree to testify against him."

Agent Carle said. "I have convinced Kathy Black to press charges and she has agreed to do so. Homer Price will be tried on the rape of Kathy Black and is to be transferred to the state prison in Georgetown, Delaware to await trial because his bail has not been made We were told to drop all the present charges on Douglas Weaver and Alfred Warrington. "

"I should also tell you that Robert Miller and Kathy Black will be married in Wilmington next Saturday evening. You should read the transcript of my last interviews with both Bob and Kathy and you will see why I am so pleased to announce their marriage plans."

"Guys we are back to square one. Who raped and killed those two girls?"

"I hope that we can get an answer to that question soon. I suggest that all of us take a copy of all of our past interviews and spend some time in reviewing them to see if we can find a clue somewhere in them."

"I am pretty confident that we are overlooking something. We must look close and forget those clues that led us to believe that Homer Price or Alfred Warrington was our man. I am afraid that we let their past history influence our decision."

"I think that Harriet's pregnancy may have something to do with her murder. Perhaps someone did not want to be charged with that fact, because of the child support that he would face. That's still the same motive that we started with."

"Alfred Warrington would still fit in that category. I realize that the DNA semen test did not match with him, but perhaps Harriet had sex with someone else prior to her death and before he killed her. Remember that Bob Miller told us that another man did sit with her at the Flagship restaurant when he got up to leave. Perhaps we need to go back to that incident. Bob Miller said he did not know who the man was, if I am correct. Bob did identify Alfred Warrington but the DNA tests indicate that Alfred is not the one who had sex with Harriet or Jeanne."

"Bill, does that DNA sample also indicate that Alfred was not the father of Harriet's fetus?"

"That a good question Chief, I will have to get that answer from the Coroner or the Forensic team. The report we have did not address that. I will have an answer to that question for you in a few hours. If it can state that the fetus was not his we can forget Alfred completely"

Bill Carle added, "Men, Alfred certainly lied to us about where he was on the night of her murder, and agent Spedden just reminded me that Bob Miller did identify Alfred as the one in the Flagship Restaurant talking to

Harriet when he left after having dinner with Harriet and at this time was the last person we know who was with Harriet. I think the chief is correct, that Alfred he is still a strong suspect, but evidently the motive that we had in suspecting Alfred is wrong, unless the DNA fetus gives us a positive match."

"And then in our last interview with him, he said that he had not dated Harriet since March. Is it possible that the Coroner or the Forensic team could determine just how old that fetus was and who was its father?"

"Wouldn't that really put Alfred back in the picture if it was about three months old? Again the DNA test may answer that question for us? He seemed determined to point out to us several times that he had not been with Harriet since March, and we know that Bob Miller told us that he sat down and talked to Harriet after he had dinner with Harriet and as he left the table. So he told us another lie. He seems to have a problem with the truth."

"Maybe he had impregnated her and was trying to avoid another expensive settlement like his family made for him with Sally Truitt. We need to get an answer to that question. Bob will you handle that?"

"Sure will, that possibility really has me thinking. I think maybe the Coroner will answer these questions for us as Bill suggested."

Chief Daley jumped into the conversation, and said. "Men you are repeating your feelings on the case, we need to wait until we hear from the Coroner and the Forensic people before we go jumping to conclusions we will have an answer very soon."

"I think we need to concentrate on those drug addicts, who came up here from Florida with Harry Black. Harriet's purse was empty and found in her car which was found abandoned in Laurel. Could they have robbed her, and then took her car to Laurel to be picked up later by Harry Black who was driving his prostitute's car while they all were in Delaware? We need a DNA test on those two men as well and I will contact our Florida Branch Office to have that done right away."

"We need to dig into their activities and a DNA study should answer their involvement status."

"What about Harry Black shouldn't he be placed in that same group?"

"Well I guess he could be, but we have reports that Harry is gay."

"I think we should still request a DNA on him anyway. I have been told that some homosexuals are bisexual."

"Yes, you are right we will proceed on all three of them. Another thing, we have never interviewed the prostitute that was in Seaford with them, perhaps we should talk with her too. Maybe she can shed some light on their activities that we are unaware of. Jack will you do those interviews for us?"

"Yes I will get on that as soon as I can determine just where they are now."

"Perhaps the murderer is married and doesn't want his wife to learn of his infidelity and with that thought

I am interested in determining if Horace Hastings could have been the one to get Harriet pregnant. His wife states that he was dating and as she put it messing with Harriet."

"Perhaps if he was the one, he may have been concerned about that pregnancy becoming known and thought that would have been very costly in his divorce settlement with his wife Helen if a claim of adultery was made against him."

Agent Spedden asked," Jack that may be a possibility and that just may answer our question as to why Jeanne Records was killed. If she was as close to Harriet, as we have been told over and over again, perhaps she was indeed raped and killed only to keep her from talking and to through us off the track by having everyone thing that a rapist was guilty of the murders."

"Even though Horace was killed by that guy from Salisbury Maryland, is it still possible to check his DNA? Do we already have Horace's DNA? His wife has told us that Horace was messing around with Harriet. Perhaps the semen was his."

Chief Daley replied, "Bill, I will check on that with their office right away and if it can be done I will order the test today."

Agent Spedden asked. "That's a good question Bill, but do you think that he was also messing around with Jeanne Records, because her DNA sample matched that found in Harriet?"

"Gosh, yes that is right, I forgot about that match.

That gives us another thing to check. Mrs. Hastings did say she thought Horace was messing around with both women. Could she be right?"

Agent Carle told the chief, "The one thing that I keep wondering about that has not been addressed yet is; just how did Harriet's car get to Laurel, Delaware? Did the murderer use it to get out of Seaford? Or was it just planted there to appear as a robbery? Perhaps the murderer of these women was indeed a stranger and used the car to get away from Seaford maybe in fact he does live in Laurel"

"Someone suggested, if I recall correctly, that perhaps the drug addicts did it. We need to see if we can prove they did or did not do it. The DNA results have the answers to whom really did it? If we find out whose DNA that is I think we will know who the murderer is."

"Chief, I think you are correct in that assessment."

The meeting was just about to break up when, a local policeman, Harry Hickman, knocked on the door and was admitted.

The officer told the team, that a woman's body had just been found no more than three miles from where the two murdered women were previously found. The body was found by a couple of boys who were exploring the area for a place to put a canoe in the Nanticoke River.

"Oh my God, who this time? Is this killing ever going to stop? Maybe we do have a serial killer in the area after all and he may not even be a member of the class. Have we been barking up the wrong tree?"

"Maybe we have been working and looking at the wrong group of people all this time. I still really think he is a member of the graduation class but we need to start looking elsewhere just as hard."

"If I am right this woman will also be a member of the class. I'm going to get to the bottom of this even if I have to put a 24 hour 7 day surveillance on every one in that class."

Agent Spedden added, "Why don't we start with an announcement that we have a suspect in this woman's murder and that an arrest will be made soon. Maybe that would cause the actual murderer to do something foolish but more important, and what I want, is that the announcement may open up some new dialog with someone."

"We certainly got them talking when we did that last time and we must remember that we have several men who could have done this, that Bill just told us about, and all but Homer were released after the DNA test report. Perhaps the DNA test is faulty or there might be a possibility that the semen was of a man other than the actual killer."

"Had the girls had sex with someone else before being killed? This new killing may have happened because the killer is under the impression that he has been cleared and he thinks he is no longer a suspect."

"I personally don't think that any of our suspects could be guilty of killing this woman. But now we have another murder and a new one to solve."

Well that's a possibility but we still have Homer Price, in custody, so we can eliminate him. That leaves us with only one suspect. Alfred Warrington. Let's put a tail on his every move."

"Well that is true but we should wait to find out all the data on this new girl before we start making assumptions. Perhaps she was killed some time ago. Until we determine who this lady is and we get those DNA reports, we cannot make any assumptions."

"We need to comb the area where this new woman was found for any clues that we may find, and have the Coroner and Forensic team estimate the date and how she was killed."

"Let's get going, we also need to do yet another series of interviews. I still think that someone out there is withholding some information that would lead us to this killer. Are they withholding information intentionally or unknowingly, that is the question. We need to concentrate on motives. There is something that is definitely motivating this killer. He may or may not be a rapist at all."

When Agents Carle and Spedden arrived at the wooded area where the body of this last girl was found murdered, the police had already closed off the area from all unofficial traffic, and a search of the area and scene was well underway.

This body, unlike the others, was not in the marsh or river. It had been found by two boys who were looking for a place to launch their canoe out of a pickup truck as was the boys that found the first murder. The Coroner, who was at the scene, stated that he felt the murder was no more than 24 hours ago but he could not confirm that until an autopsy was completed.

The woman was fully clothed and there was no indication that she had been molested, but that would have to wait until the Coroner had the body in his lab to determine that for sure. An opened condom packet was found on the ground as was an unused and unrolled condom.

The team found drug items at the scene, and fresh tire tracks which were copied to a plaster mold and sent to the forensic lab. This killing had the marks of a drug overdose and a wallet taken from a woman's purse contained a large sum of money and several vials of narcotics. It was apparent that this woman was an addict.

A photo ID found on the Florida driver's license taken from the wallet indicated that the body was indeed that of the dead woman. The name on the driver's license was S. Grace Marvel and her address was listed as Tampa, Florida.

Her address immediately caused the team to suspect a connection with Harry Black.

A review of the high school year book had failed to list a girl by the name of Grace and all girls in the yearbook with a name that started with S were definitely not of the woman found in the wooded area.

The FBI team then contacted the Tampa police for information on the persons living at the address on the license. They were told that there was a woman who lived at that address named Grace Marvel, and that she was not at that address but reported to be with a local drug dealer with the name of Harry Black. The girl had been arrested three times on charges of prostitution and five times for various drug violations.

"Ye Gads, is Harry back on drugs and could he possibly be back here in Delaware? Could we have missed something when he was interviewed in Tampa?" asked agent Carle.

"If he is back in Seaford he may possibly have made contact with his old friend, Oliver Hill. Harry told us that he had sold drugs to Oliver when he was in Seaford, prior to the reunion. Oliver was his lover when he was in high school. And it was mentioned that he had made prostitutes available for Oliver when they were in high school. I think we need to check back on both Harry and Oliver immediately. Let's go see Oliver."

When they arrived at Oliver's residence, there was no one at home. A neighbor was asked if she knew whether Oliver had any guest visiting from Florida. The neighbor replied, "I'm not sure that his guests are still here or not; but they have been partying over there for about three days. I think they are all on drugs."

"Were the visitors in a car with Florida tags?"

"They were in a van not a car. It was a beat up old grey but rusted Dodge van, with Florida tags on it. Oliver's truck is gone. He has an almost new red Chevy pickup with a cover over the back which is white."

"All of his guests left several days ago except a woman.

She was staying with Oliver after the van left. She came with the van, but we haven't seen her since yesterday morning. She and Oliver left here together yesterday afternoon but only Oliver came back. The lady was not with him. I guess they are all gone now."

Agent Clarke, put out a wanted notice alert for Harry Black and Oliver Hill on suspicion of a mysterious death with the city and state police using the identification and information given to him by the neighbor.

It was less than an hour before the Delaware State Police had the van and it's passengers in custody at the State Police Barracks and they were jailed in the Bridgeville, Delaware State Police barracks.

They were all arrested for possession of a controlled substance, and Harry Black, Johnnie James and Henry Walker were all being held as suspects in the death of a woman in Seaford, Delaware.

Harry Black was also charged with driving under the influence of a controlled substance. The owner of the car on the Florida vehicle registration was not in the car when it was stopped on the southbound lane of U.S Highway 13, just south of Greenwood, Delaware.

The tires of the van were removed and casts were made of each tire for comparison with those found at the death scene. None of the cast molds matched those found at the scene and each mold from the tires on the van indicated considerable more wear than those from the scene.

The state police lab determined that the casts made at

the scene when compared with those from the van were not from the van.

Agents Carle and Spedden interviewed the three men at the state prison in Georgetown where they had been sent.

"Harry, I have a report from Agent Carson in Florida that you had promised him that you were going into rehab, and here you are back in Delaware being held for drug possession and driving under the influence of a controlled substance, what happened?"

"Well Mr. Carle, I did try. I had hope, but no one would hire me to play music and it became a matter of money. I had none and the only way I could find any was to start selling again and I soon became my own best customer."

"I'm hooked again. They told me that I was a suspect in the death of a woman. I haven't killed anybody. You have to believe me."

"Harry where is the girl that left Florida with you?"

"You mean Gracie. She is with my old friend Oliver Hill down in Seaford. She is working for us and she keeps us all in drug money. I'm gay, you probably know that, and I find a few men once in awhile that pay me for giving them relief too."

"You mean that you are her pimp?"

"Well I guess you could say that; but she and I are friends and we both need money for our habits. We pimp for each other. That's why we left her with Oliver."

"Harry, you will have to find a new bimbo. Grace was found dead in Seaford yesterday afternoon.

Why did you guys kill her?"

"Kill her? Oh my God no, we left her with Oliver in Seaford, while we went to Dover, Delaware to get some more drugs."

"We had nothing to do with that. We all loved Gracie, she kept us in money. Please believe me -- just ask Oliver he will tell you about what she did or where she went after we left."

"The last time the three of us saw Gracie was the day we left to go up to Dover. She stayed behind with Oliver and was to wait there until we picked her up when we got back. We could have used her in Dover too as it turned out. Oliver promised to give us money if we would leave her with him for several days and if she would have sex with him."

"We did that the last time we were in Seaford too and he paid us with no problem. Gracie didn't like making love with him but we needed the money."

"I offered to take care of Oliver but he refused, he wanted a woman. He is not gay and preferred women. I told that FBI man in Florida about that."

"Yes, we have a record of that conversation. Oliver was not at home when we went to see him after Grace's murder. Do you have any idea where he is now? Was he at home when you left Seaford and was Grace still with him when you all left?"

"Isn't he in Seaford? When we left Seaford they were

both in bed having sex. We watched them for awhile. What a sight that was. If I had a camera I could really sell those pictures, Oliver is like a wild man when he's on a woman."

"He doesn't get the opportunity to have a woman too often because he's so damn ugly. We did that the last time we were in Seaford too and he paid us $200 with no problem."

"Harry, are you telling me that Grace was with you when you were in Seaford to attend the reunion in May? You didn't mention that in your interview in Florida with Mr. Carson."

"Mr. Carson didn't ask me about Gracie. Yes she was with us and like I said, she stayed with Oliver when we went up to Dover City to get some drugs one eveneing. After we got the drugs with Oliver's money, we picked her up at his house and drove to North Carolina and on to Florida."

"Well we are going to ask your friends what happened. You better hope that they tell us the same story."

"One more question Harry, why did you drive that red convertible of Harriet's down to Laurel?"

"What red convertible? I didn't drive any car to Laurel."

"Oh, then it must have been one of your buddies, I will ask them."

"There's no need to do that, the whole time we were in Seaford they were with me all the time. Whose car was it?"

"It belonged to Harriet O'Brien and she had been robbed. All her money was gone."

"Well it wasn't any of us."

"We kind of think it was. We are checking on some clues we found in the car."

Of course the investigators had no clues and were just trying to get Harry to say something that would point to one of his friends or himself.

Agent Carle then asked the jail guard to bring him the other prisoners, one at a time, and to keep them away from each other and away from Harry until the interviews were all completed.

The two other men were asked the same questions as were asked Harry, and their response was basically identical to Hurry's responses.

They all stated that they had not seen Grace since they left her with Oliver. One of them even retold Carle about Oliver being in bed with Grace when the three of them left for Dover.

When agent Carle returned to Seaford, he was told that Oliver Hill had still not returned home and his whereabouts were still unknown. Two days later he still had not come home, and a wanted poster was disseminated to all offices for his arrest as a suspected murderer of Harriet O'Brien, and Jeanne Records and as a suspect in the mysterious death of S. Grace Marvel.

A description of his pickup truck and its Delaware license number was provided. There was no picture available but a write up on the deformity in his eyes was described.

A meeting of the investigation team was called and the members were told to continue conducting their interviews until it was determined if Oliver Hill had committed all three murders. It was pointing in that direction at the moment.

Chief Daley told them that he would be giving the newspaper reporters an interview that afternoon and was going to tell them that the police were asking for help in locating Oliver Hill for questioning on the death of a Florida woman while she was visiting in Seaford.

He also said that he would add that they were seeking information on a red convertible sports car that was abandoned in the church parking lot in Laurel that belonged to one of the women murdered in Seaford at the time of a class reunion.

It was his hope that perhaps someone may have witnessed the car being parked in the lot. It was parked in a spot that could be viewed from any direction.

He told his team members, "It appears to me as if someone wanted that car to be found."

He was hoping that the message he would give the press would reach someone that could help them find Oliver or to possibly give them information on Oliver or about the car left in Laurel.

Again his use of the newspapers provided them with additional information on both Oliver and the girl.

Norris Allen had called the police on the telephone

and told them that Oliver and Grace came in a bar on High Street and were drinking. Oliver left her in the bar after they had a loud argument.

Agent Carle met with the informant and asked him for the details.

"Mr. Allen you say that they were having an argument. Do you know what the argument was about?"

"I don't know exactly what prompted the argument. But I am pretty sure that the girl was soliciting some of the men in the bar and he didn't like that."

"What do you mean by soliciting some of the men?"

"In my opinion, I think she was a prostitute. She was drinking beer and going from table to table and teasing the men. At several tables she joined the men and several of them were taking liberties with her and she loved it. Poor Oliver did not appreciate that at all."

"Did she leave with any of the men?"

"Yes she did; but not until after Oliver left."

"Are you telling me that Oliver left without her?"

"Yes, and she left the bar after a few minutes with a man that I didn't know. I was in the bar until it closed, and they didn't come back. After they left, we were all laughing and talking about him. I remember telling Joe Larson that the guy better have a condom or he was going to get more than he was going to pay for."

"Can you give me a description of the man?"

"Let me think. He was white of course and I would guess about twenty to twenty five years of age. He had tattoos on both of his arms, lots of tattoos actually on each arm. He had black hair but it was cut short like a crew cut."

"He appeared to be very muscular. I thought he may have been a construction type or at least someone who worked outside. I wouldn't want to tangle with him."

"Was he alone in the bar or was he with other men when she approached him?

"He came in the bar with two or three other men before she and Oliver came in and they were all in a booth drinking beer. It must have been three men because she was sitting in the booth with the men."

"I am sure the men all knew each other and I would have thought that they all worked together because they all had dusty clothes on. They were covered with plaster, paint, cement, or something like that, and it was all over their clothes. All of them left shortly after the woman and the first manleft."

"John Ryder told all of us still in the bar; I think there's going to be a "gang bang" tonight and we all agreed and laughed."

"Did you by chance see what they left the bar in, like a van, truck, or a car?"

"No, I didn't leave the bar until it closed."

"Do you go to the bar often?"

"Yes, almost every Friday night. I am sure that it was a Friday night."

"I was in the bar after work when Oliver and that girl came in."

"Well then if those men were regulars, you would have probably known them."

"Yes, I think so. I had never seen these men before and even Grover asked me who they were."

"Who is Grover?"

"Oh sorry, he owns the bar and is also the bartender, Grover Johnson."

The Coroner's report revealed that Grace had definitely been sexually active and that she was most likely a prostitute as the Florida police had mentioned when she was identified. DNA samples were taken and had been sent off for an analysis.

Later that afternoon, agent Carle got a telephone call from William Preston asking to see him regarding the death of Grace Marvel and agent Carle agreed to meet with him at the police headquarters in thirty minutes.

"Mr. Carle, my name is William Preston. I have information on the death of the prostitute that was mentioned in the Morning News yesterday as being murdered."

Mr. Carle that girl was not murdered. She died of a drug overdose by her own hands."

"Mr. Preston how do you know she was not murdered and how she died?"

"Well last Friday night a few of us men that are working on the new elementary school building were in Grover's Bar on High Street drinking beer when this girl approached our table and asked us if we wanted to have some fun."

"We knew that she was a prostitute and that she was really high on drink or drugs at the time. We had enough beer to take her up on her offer. She asked for fifty dollars and we told her that was too much. She agreed to twenty each if we all did it."

"She said she needed a hundred dollars but agreed to the $80.00from the four of us. Fred Baker said he would go to the pharmacy and get some condoms. I can tell you that there was no way that I would have gone with that woman without a condom."

"We drove our van east on the road to Georgetown and found a wooded area where we planned to have sex with this woman, but she said that she first needed to get herself ready, It turned out that she was injecting a drug of some sort. I don't know why; because she was as high as one could be already."

"She took her purse and went outside our van to inject the drug. We were all waiting in front of the van and when she did not return in about ten to fifteen minutes, I walked to the rear of the car and she was lying on the ground. Dead as could be. We got scared and pulled her off the roadway and left in a hurry."

"Then when the newspaper came out and stated that another woman's body had been found murdered, I knew that there were people in Grover's Bar that knew we left with her and we would immediately become suspects and I knew that she was not murdered."

"Honestly, Mr. Carle that is exactly what happened. We never touched the woman. I knew that I had to come forward and tell you what happened. I am not married but the three others are all married men. We don't want this to make the newspapers."

At the team meeting the next morning, Carle advised the team that evidently the Coroner's report was accurate. There was no evidence of abuse to the woman, and it was confirmed that she died of an overdose of the drug found in her purse.

The newspaper reported in their evening edition that Grace had died from a self injected overdose of a drug and that a drug dealer and two companions all of Tampa, Florida were arrested on possession of a controlled substance, with an intent to sell and were awaiting trial. It also reported that officials in Seaford reported that the death of the Florida woman was not related to the reunion murders.

"Oliver Hill has still not come home and he is still wanted for questioning. I am sure we will have him soon. We must not stop with our ongoing investigations; we have nothing to indicate that Oliver has anything to do with the cases we are working on."

"The thing that I feel must be answered first is to determine if there is any connection between our two open murders. The same old question, why was the second girl, Jeanne Records murdered? We do know that she was raped, but she was Harriet's best friend and almost everyone we interviewed stated that Harriet and Jeanne were almost always together and that lets me think that she was killed because of what she knew about Harriet."

"Perhaps the rape was done only to throw us off the real reason. So let's start interviewing other friends. We do know that Horace was killed by Larry Adams, but we also know that Horace was involved with Harriet. Let' see if we can find out what Jeanne knew about Harriet and Horace that may have caused her to be silenced."

An anonymous call was received at police quarters from a woman that simply stated, "Jeanne Records was killed because she knew that Horace and Harriet were having an affair that would hurt Horace's chance of a favorable divorce award because his wife Helen could have claimed adultery charges, which would result favorably with the judge. She then hung up without giving her name,

Unknown to the caller, the call was traced to Barbara Strong, a member of the class of 1984 who was in attendance at the reunion. She had been interviewed earlier by agent Spedden, but she had previously given no testimony about Harriet and Jeanne.

She did mention in her earlier interview that Horace was a close friend of Harriet and Jeanne, as did almost everyone in the class.

She told agent Spedden in that interview, that Horace had become very wealthy in his chicken business and money may have played a part in the reason he was killed.

NINETEEN

AGENT CARLE ARRIVED at Mrs. Strong house on schedule. He did not mention that he was aware that she had called the office earlier.

"Mrs. Strong, we are going over all of the interviews we did some time ago, to check up on some testimony we have gathered, and in doing a review of our earlier interviews with all their classmates, it was mentioned by several of them that perhaps Jeanne Records, may have been murdered to keep her from telling something that Harriet knew. Do you think that her murder was for that reason?"

"As I told you before, Horace had become very wealthy in his farming and chicken operations, and possibly he may have been killed for his money. The newspaper said that he was killed by a man from Salisbury who was

228

trying to get Horace out of the way so he could marry Helen and get her money."

"Before I read that in the paper, I was thinking that Horace may have killed Jeanne because he was running out on Helen and messing with Harriet. I had heard from several people, including Jeanne that Horace was having an affair with Harriet, and that Horace and Helen were getting a divorce. Jeanne told me that Horace was claiming that Helen had committed adultery."

"The truth of the matter; however, was that Horace was the one committing adultery and Helen herself told me that she was seeing that man from Salisbury, but she was not having an affair with him. He was helping her in her financial affairs to protect her interests."

"As it has turned out according to the paper, he was planning on filling his own pockets. Poor Helen was so easily mislead."

"I was thinking at that time just perhaps, Horace had killed Jeanne, or had hired someone to kill Jeanne to keep his affair from becoming public and if his affair was to become known, he would most likely stand to lose a lot of money in the divorce settlement, but why was Harriet killed? All he had to do was just quit the relationship."

"Please understand that all of this is just my thoughts on the matter, I have no proof to back up my thoughts, but it is the only thing that I can think of as to why Jeanne may have been killed."

"I don't believe for a minute, that rape was the reason she was killed. I really think that she was killed to cover up the true reason that Harriet was killed."

"Could Horace's death be just a coincidence that is confusing the real story? I do know one thing I don't think that Harriet was really raped. Was there evidence of that or could she have had sex earlier? I know Harriet and she would have fought the guy to her death before she would let a man rape her. She could have bettered half the boys in our class anyway. She was very athletic and strong."

"I understand Mrs. Strong, and we will get to the bottom of all of this and we appreciate your thoughts on the matter, Can you recall just when Jeanne told you about Horace having an affair with Harriet?"

"Yes, it was the night that a meeting of the reunion committee was held. I did not attend the meeting but Jeanne told me the next morning what was decided at the meeting in the grocery the next morning and that is when she told me that Horace and Helen were getting divorced and that Horace was going to marry Harriet as soon as the divorce was settled and when I questioned her about that she told me that Harriet had told her just the night before that she was pregnant with Horace's child."

"Both were claiming adultery. Helen told me after Harriet was killed; that the man she had been seen with was simply a man helping her with her divorce and she was not having an affair with him. He was just helping her to protect her interests in the family business."

"It then dawned on me that perhaps Horace did kill both Harriet and Jeanne. Killing first Harriet because he didn't want to lose money in his divorce, and then

Jeanne because perhaps he knew Jeanne knew about the pregnancy."

Agent Carle acted like he was surprised that Harriet was pregnant and that he was not aware of the other information that she had told him about although the only thing that came out of the interview with Mrs. Strong was that Horace was said to have been the one who impregnated Harriet. That was a new twist.

Agent Carle had lunch with Helen after he arrived back at the station to file his report, and asked Helen to confirm Mrs. Strong's comment about having a talk with Jeanne in which she told her about Horace and Harriet having an affair and that she had told Mrs. Strong that she was seeing a man but only to help her with her financial affairs.

Helen confirmed those statements. He did not mention about Horace being mentioned as the one who impregnated Harriet.

Following lunch, agent Carle received a call on his cell phone and was told that Oliver had returned home and that he was in custody at the police station.

"Helen, I must leave now, but how about dinner this evening?"

"That's a deal, but how about coming to my house and I will cook us a great dinner. I will stop at the grocers and pick up a couple steaks and some franks and ground beef for the children, and we can cook them on the grill?"

"Great, I will do the cooking on the grill. Pick up a six pack of beer. Better still make it two six packs, and how about calling Kathy and Robert to see if they will join us. I think that they will be going to Wilmington in the next few days. I need to talk to them about the wedding arrangements."

"That's a great idea. I will call them when I get home. If they can't make it I will call you, but we can have dinner anyway."

When Carle arrived at the station, agent Spedden was just starting to question Oliver Hill and Carle joined in on the questioning.

"Oliver, you were last seen with the lady that was traveling with you, Grace Marvel in Grover's Bar on High Street. We have been told that you left the bar after having an argument with her. Is that true, and can you tell us what the argument was about?"

"Grace is that her name? Yes, I was at the bar with her. She and I had gone there to have a few drinks before we went back to my house."

"I suppose that you already know that she was a prostitute friend of Harry Black. I had paid Harry a hundred and fifty dollars to leave her with me while he went to Dover."

"I suppose that he was going there to buy some drugs; at least, that was what he told me he was going there for. He agreed to let her stay with me. Grace, if that was her name, and I had sex several times."

"All was going well until we ran out of beer and decided to go in town to get some more. We decided to stop at Grover's for a couple beers before we went to the liquor store. Grace went to the bathroom and when she came back, I knew that she had taken some drugs because she changed – she was happy, laughing and started flirting with all the men in the bar."

"That's when the argument started. I told her that I had paid Harry for her until he got back from Dover. She told me that we had had sex twice already and that was what I paid for. She said that she was finished with me."

"She found a group of men and joined them leaving me alone. I went to their table and they told me to get lost. There were three of them and they were all on the make for her. I suppose that they all went with her but I don't know that for sure. I was mad and left."

Agent Carle then asked, "Well that explains what the argument was about; but why did you disappear. Why didn't you just go home? Where did you go?"

"I did go home but when I got there, I was so mad that I decided that I didn't want to be there when she came back, or when Harry came back. I feared what I would do to them so I drove to Ocean City and found another prostitute and stayed there with her until today?"

"Why are you questioning me? I have nothing to do with their drug business."

"Oliver, Grace was found dead East of Seaford, the day after you were last seen with her?"

"Oh damn, you got to be kidding, I had nothing to do with that believe me. I charged my motel room in Ocean City. That will prove that I was there. I'm sure Grover saw me leave the bar without her. Please ask him."

"Was it those three men who were trying to make her? Yes, that's probably it. I bet one of them killed her."

"No, Oliver, she was not killed she died of a drug overdose."

"Oh, that would make more sense. You had me scared for a minute. I thought you suspected me of killing her. Harry was always the one who injected whatever it was in her. She was already high enough and probably didn't know just how much to inject like Harry did."

"Oliver, we do believe however that you may have had something to do with the deaths of Harriet O'Brien and Jeanne Records."

"Well you are certainly mistaken I haven't killed anyone. Why would you think that I did that?"

"Because we know that you frequent prostitutes and because you lied to us."

"That is not a reason to kill anyone. I can buy what I want from a woman. When did I lie to you?"

"That's true, but it is just as easy to rape one and then kill her to keep her from telling on you. You lied to us when you said you had not seen Harriet in a long time. You were seen talking to her just the day she was murdered."

"Mr. Carle, are you charging me with those murders? I know that I have associated myself with some drug users and dealers, and prostitutes, but I haven't killed anyone. You have got to believe me. If I told you that I had not talked with Harriet than I must have forgotten that."

"When and where was I seen talking to her? I just

can't remember that at all; but if I did, I can't remember it. Hey wait a minute I do remember talking to her now. But I wasn't the one doing the talking it was Harriet that was doing all the talking. She was trying to talk me into going to the reunion. I think it was in front of the Deli."

"No, Oliver we are not charging you with anything and we do hope that you were not involved with them, but we are thinking that you may have some information on who actually did the rape and murders. "Can't you help us find the guy? Is there a possibility that Harry or his friends did it? You better tell us what you know to clear yourself."

"Mr. Carle, I can't speak for the guys with Harry, but I think I told you before, that Harry is gay. I am pretty certain that he himself did not rape the girls. But at any rate, believe me Mr. Carle I know nothing about those murders."

"Ok, Oliver we are not going to hold you, but you are not to leave this area without your letting us know where you are going. Is that agreeable?"

"Yes. Thank you and if I can think or hear of anything to help you, I will surely let you know."

"Oh, one more thing Oliver what can you tell me about Harriet's red convertible?"

"Sure, what do you want to know about it? It's a very nice car for certain. She was in that car at the Deli when she tried to convince me into going to the reunion. She was telling me how she liked it. It was late at night as I recall, and she had the top down."

"Can you tell me if Harry or either of his two friends mentioned anything about her car, or perhaps explained why it was parked in Laurel?"

"No, I never heard them mention anything about her car and they never had it as far as I know. What took it in Laurel? I have no idea about how it got there or who could have driven it there if she didn't do it herself."

Later at the station, Bob Spedden was reading over Carle's interview with Oliver. "Bill, why did you ask him about Harriet's car that was found in Laurel?"

"Well, Bob, I am thoroughly convinced that the car holds the answer as to who murdered Harriet, and probably Jeanne. I just can't get it out of my mind. Why would it be driven to Laurel? Who drove it down there and why?"

"You may be right about that. We need to pursue those questions. The thought just came to me that perhaps an accomplice drove the car. Is there a possibility that there could have been two persons involved in these murders and the rape?"

"I think that may be a possibility, but I am still concerned about Alfred Warrington. I am going to talk with him again in the morning. He lied to us and he certainly went on the defensive the minute we told him we were investigating Harriet's murder."

Bob and Kathy arrived at Helen's house before Bill arrived. Kathy's son Norman was with them and joined Helen's two children in visiting the farm animals. Helen's farm manager, Steve Cockran, saddled up the pony for the children to ride, and stayed with them as they put the pony through its paces.

Norman had never ridden a horse but with Steve's help, he was soon taking his place in line riding the pony every third turn.

Bob filled the outdoor grill with charcoal and soon had the embers just where he wanted them to start cooking the steaks, franks, and a few hamburgers. Bill arrived and scolded Bob by telling him "that's my job" and Bob replied that was Ok with him, he would rather be the beer tester anyway and took a beer from the cooler and said "I better get on with the testing."

While Bill and Robert were cooking the meat, the ladies were in the kitchen and Helen said, "Kathy, I am so happy that you and Robert are finally going to get married and I am so happy that you want my daughter to be your flower girl. She is so excited you chose her."

"You two will certainly be a great couple. I hope that you will have a child right away and that will make you a family quicker than anything. I do hope that you have a better marriage than Horace and I had, and I know you will."

"We started off happy enough and I think that Horace did love me, but all that changed after Horace became so successful. The more money Horace made the more we started drifting apart. Horace was away from home more and more, and I suspected that when he quit making love with me over two years ago he was having an affair. I began to think that perhaps he married me for my parent's money that they gave us to get started."

"Some of my friends kept telling me that they had seen Horace and Harriet together but never did any of them tell me anything to let me know that they were indeed having an affair. Harriet and Horace were always close friends and she still spoke to me every time we met."

"I was sure that it was not Harriet that he was seeing but I thought it might have been Jeanne. I remembered from school days that she was telling all of us that she was in love with Horace. The problem was she was always in love with every new boy she dated."

"Like I said, Horace was certainly ignoring me. He began sleeping in the guest room. Then he went to his boat to sleep. My suspicion was confirmed, when Jeanne Records told me that Harriet and Horace were indeed having an affair after, I convinced her to tell me the truth and asked her if she was the one. She told me that Horace was dating several women and that she had been out with him herself, but she said that she and Horace were not having sex. I then confronted Horace about his behavior and he denied the charge."

"I knew he was lying and that is when I met Larry Adams and asked him if he would tell me how to protect my property rights in a divorce settlement. Larry had just won a divorce from his wife. I wanted out of Horace's life. He suggested that I should try to catch Horace and that is why I took Larry to the reunion."

"I approached Larry because I knew that he and his

wife had just gone through a divorce and he was what I thought to be a successful business man."

"Of course that turned out to be a bad mistake because Horace started to tell everyone that it was I who was committing adultery."

"That was certainly a lie. I did have dinner with Larry several times but only to discuss my financial concerns. I offered Larry some money if he would help me with my divorce but he said that was not necessary."

"I was aware that he was attracted to me after the third or fourth time we ate together, but I surely was not attracted to him in any way. I must admit that I did kiss him goodnight on several occasions; but that is all they were, just a quick goodnight kiss. Evidently he thought otherwise."

"I told Jeanne Records that she was right when she told me that Horace and Harriet were having an affair."

"Helen, did you tell Mr. Carle all of this?"

"I'm not sure if I told him all of what I said or not, why do you ask?"

"Helen, I asked that because I have not heard him mention that you ever had a conversation with Jeanne Records. I know that he is trying his best to determine why these girls were both killed."

"Well, feel free to tell him anything that I have mentioned to you. I do know that he was looking for people who had talked to Jeanne just before her death, but my conversation with Jeanne was at least a month or more ago. I will try to remember all I just told you this evening. If it will help close all these murders I am more than anxious to bring them to a close."

"I must admit that I will hate to see Bill leave when all of this is resolved. I sure do enjoy his presence. I don't know if her told you or not, but we knew each other in college and I was dating him until he moved to Tennessee and after he left, I started dating Horace and we married in our junior year at the university. "

"I noticed that Helen, I think that he is attracted to you as well. He would make a good catch for you Helen. I think he is a wonderful man of course I am prejudiced because he brought Bob back to me."

"I'm attracted to him too but I'm not quite ready for anything like that just now. I dated him for almost a year when we were at Delaware together. He had to move when his parents moved to Tennessee and I was broken hearted. He had to move with them because he said he could not afford to live in the dorms."

"I have a lot of decisions to make with the farm and the poultry operations before I can think of another man but I do know my children need a father to grow up with. Of course, I don't know how Bill would take having to help raise two children. I plan to start teaching. I would love to work with children with learning difficulties."

Bob came in the house and told the ladies the steaks were ready and the ladies carried their salads, macaroni and cheese, and fresh corn on the cob outside to a picnic table and all the things needed to have a perfect picnic meal.

The children came running when called, and Steve the farm manager who had been caring for the children was asked to join them, and he accepted, a hamburger, a can of beer and an ear of corn and grabbed a seat at the table with the children.

All were seated and Robert offered a blessing for the food. Helen got Bill's attention; and told him that he should remind her later to tell him something about Jeanne Records. Bill said is it something that we should discuss later and she said yes.

During the picnic Bill was asked several general questions about his progress. Bob asked him. "Bill, did you ever find out how Harriet's red convertible got to Laurel."

"Not yet Bob, but we are of the opinion that it was driven there by Harriet's murderer. We feel now that Harriet may have been driving the car herself when she met the murderer. We feel he was well known to her, and he may have had an accomplice after the murder in helping him to dispose of her car."

"Then again, the murderer could possibly live in Laurel and drove it to Laurel after the murder. We just have found no leads that lets' us determine out how that car got there."

"No one seems to know anything about that car even as visible as it really was. There are not many red sports cars around like it. We are doing some questioning of some persons in Laurel now in hopes that we can find someone that saw the car being parked in Laurel. That's enough about the case. Let's get back to the picnic. Bob do you and Steve, want to play a game of horse shoes?"

After the picnic was over and all were sitting around with full bellies, Bob and Kathy told Bill and Helen that they were to be married in Seaford, the coming Sunday following the regular church service and that her furniture was to be placed in storage until they found a new home in Wilmington.

Linda, the four year old daughter of Helen told everyone, "Momma said that she was going to marry Mr. Carle."

"Linda, I never said any such thing. Why would you say such a thing?"

"Yes you did mom, I asked you last night when I went to bed, if you were ever going to get us a new daddy and you said that you would someday if you found the right man, and I heard you tell Miss Black that you were attracted to him. I think Mr. Carle is the right man."

"Well Mr. Carle is a very nice man Linda, but I think we need a lot of time to get things here on the farm straightened out before we start looking for a new dad, Beside Mr. Carle, might not want to be your new daddy."

"Linda, you tell your mother that I will consider being your new daddy, but like your mother said, we need time before we jump into that. I'm not a farmer and all I know about farming is how to eat the crops and then only if somebody else cooks them."

"Mr. Carle, we don't grow any crops to eat except in

our little garden, we grow corn and soybeans to feed the chickens. We do raise chickens but we sell all of them to Mr. Perdue. You don't have to know nothing Mr. Steve takes care of the farm. Don't you Mr. Cockran? I want you as my new daddy."

"Well then, maybe I will consider your offer, but you better talk about that with your mother later."

It was beginning to get dark and Robert suggested to Kathy that they should be going home.

After they left, Bill asked Helen, "You asked me to remind you about Jeanne Records. What's that all about?"

"When Kathy and I were talking, I mentioned to her about a conversation that I had with Jeanne Records about a month or so before she was murdered, she asked me if I had told you, and I can't recall if I did or not. She said I should tell you anyway."

"I was telling her that after I married Horace that all was going well until he became so successful. The more money Horace made it seems that we started drifting apart. I told her Horace was away from home more and more and I suspected that he was having an affair when he quit making love with me about two years ago."

"I told her that some of my friends kept telling me that they had seen Horace and Harriet together but not one of them ever let me know that they were actually having an affair."

"I put two and two together and soon figured that Horace and Jeanne were having sex. He was certainly ignoring me in that area. I knew that Horace and Harriet were seeing each other but I thought nothing of that. They have been close friends since school days. I simply thought that was the case. I thought it was Jeanne. She was always throwing herself to Horace all the time, even when we were just married."

"When I asked Jeanne if she and Horace were having an affair, she told me that it was Harriet not her who was having the affair. She admitted that she had been out with Horace but there was no sex. I had convinced her to tell me the truth."

"That is when Kathy asked me if I had told you that Harriet and Horace were having sex and I could not remember if I mentioned that to you or not. Did I tell you that?"

"I will check the transcript to see, but I don't recall you saying Horace and Harriet were having sex, but. I know that you did mention that Jeanne had told you that Horace was seeing Harriet. The thing that I am concerned about now is that I wonder if Jeanne told Horace that you knew about their having sex. That is a very new important disclosure."

"Why is that such an important disclosure?"

"Because it may be a motive for her being killed that has had us buffaloed all this time. Just what did Jeanne tell Horace or anyone else? Maybe she was killed to shut her up over something she knew about Harriet's death."

"Why would that be a motive or reason for her having been killed?"

"Well Helen, for now it's best to let us make that determination, but it does give us something to search for as we continue our investigation. Harriet was pregnant. Right now I have a question for you. Did you really tell Kathy you were attracted to me?"

"Yes, I did in a way. I told her that I would hate to see you leave when all of this is over. I told her that I enjoy your company and that I was attracted to you and that I was in love with you when we dated in college. Remember?"

" Bill you must remember that Horace has only been dead for a little over three months now and I have a lot to handle at this time."

"I have been thinking that I just might turn all of the poultry business over to his father and brothers. They are all as hurt and upset about all of this as I am, and they are my children's grandparents and uncles. I don't want them taken out of my children's life. I feel that they can arrange to make some kind of financial arrangements for my children and me."

"Helen, I think that would be the perfect thing to do. It certainly would take a lot of responsibility off your shoulders. I want you to know, as you put it, I am attracted to you also and at this time I would like to be your -- just how should I say it -- your boyfriend. I enjoy being with you too and I am not ready to make any kind of commitment at this time either."

"My job takes me away from home for long periods of

time and I never know where I will be going or how long I will have to be away from home."

"The life of an FBI agent is a tough life for a family man, but sometime in the future, I hope to be permanently assigned to head up a branch office, and I could then think about some permanency. Yes, Helen, I do love you."

The next morning, Bob Spedden and Bill Carle, went to Georgetown to interview Alfred Warrington again.

"Alfred, we find it necessary to ask you some questions about your relationship with Harriet Obrien and Jeanne Records. You gave us some false information the last time we interviewed you."

"Yes, and I am sorry about that but I was scared and I told you that after you checked on my alibi. I was afraid that you would use my paternity suit settlement of years ago, and accuse me of killing those women to prevent my having to pay for the child support that I had to do back in my senior year."

"Alfred the problem we have now is that you told us that you had not dated Harriet since last March, but we have been told you were seen with her as recently as June just the day or two before the reunion."

"I didn't say that I had not seen her, what I said was that I had not been on a date with her, and that is the truth."

"Then tell me when you were last seen with Harriet and the purpose of your coming to Seaford from Georgetown to talk with her. We know you met her in the Flagship restaurant the night she was killed. Did she initiate your getting together to talk or did you initiate the meeting?"

"Well, neither one of us did really I stopped at the Flagship Restaurant to have a few drinks in the bar and met Jeanne there. She came over to sit on the stool next to me and she told me that Harriet had told her that she was pregnant and that she was going to get married. She did not tell me who the father was but Jeanne asked me, if I was the father."

"I told her absolutely not. I told Jeanne that I was not the father."

"Jeanne apologized to me and said well I just assumed it was you. Then Horace must be the father. Then she asked me if I thought that Horace was the father? She seemed to be upset that Harriet did not tell her who it was."

"After I left Jean in the bar, I went into the restaurant's dining room, and saw Harriet having dinner with some man. He was just leaving and Harriet asked if I had a few minutes to talk. I sat down and she told me that she was pregnant. I told her yes, I know."

"I got up from the table and left. I never saw Harriet again."

"Alfred, you know that we were looking for anyone who had talked to either Harriet or Jeanne, Why didn't you tell us about this earlier?"

"Because I thought that you were thinking that I was involved with their murders in view of my past and I just didn't want to get involved in that matter."

TWENTY

A MEETING OF THE team was called for the purpose of following up on the fact that Harriet and Horace was having an affair, and that Jeanne Records had told Helen about that as well as Alfred Warrington.

The transcript of Carle's talk with Alfred was also read and discussed. Chief Daley was happy and told the team that, "It looks like we are about to settle all these riddles. Let's dig into all the data we have and determine just which one of our suspects is the guilty one."

"Men, we now have a positive motive for the murder of Jeanne Records. That motive would be to "shut her up" and the other motive of course was to prevent her from telling us who raped her and who may have killed Harriet. We need to find out if Jeanne told anyone about that affair other then Helen and Alfred, and we need to check into her activities a little. Did she date anyone regularly, where did she go for pleasure, any bars, or the like? Was she after Horace too?"

"I feel at this time, that we may have been thinking correctly on the reason for Jeanne's death. SDimply to shut her up, and I will contact the Coroner again to establish if there were any signs of a struggle on Harriet's clothing or body. I know he said that she had no evidence of being raped, but I wonder if there were any signs of abuse."

"Can he positively state that she was or was not raped in court?"

"If I recall correctly I think his report stated merely that she had intercourse with someone before she was murdered, and that she was strangled. Have we ever found anything that may have been used to strangle these women?"

"I also want to find out if there was a DNA study on Horace. We know now that Horace and Harriet were having sex and I am wondering if that semen sample on Harriet was from Horace and just whose DNA may be found in that fetus."

"Yes, we do need a DNA test on Horace, but we must also remember that the first DNA test told us that the DNA on both Harriet and Jeanne was a match." Could Horace or anyone else we know about, have been screwing both those women?"

"Have we looked for something like a wire in any of the suspect's cars or at their residence?"

"Yes, that does put a different emphasis on this case doesn't it, so until we get that DNA report we need to do some more interviews with the class members or friends and see if we can find anything of interest on Jeanne, but don't forget that there is still a possibility that their deaths were by a rapist from outside the class members.

"We still have a DNA sample that has not been tied to anyone."

"There was a rape in Delmar, Maryland just about fifteen miles south of us in July but the rapist was apprehended. He was only 18 years old and he raped his girlfriend of several years with whom he had sex with many times."

Agent Carle interviewed one of Jeanne's reported close friends, Thelma Webster, whose previous interview mentioned that Jeanne was one of her closest friend, and told him earlier that she could think of no reason why anyone would have killed Harriet unless she was raped, and that she would have put up quite a battle if she had been raped.

"Mrs. Webster, when we last talked you mentioned that Jeanne Records was one of your closest friends was that true?'

"Yes, Mr. Carle, we were the best of friends and have been since our school days. Neither one of us has married as of yet, and we have double dated many times."

"We have just learned from a reliable source that Jeanne told someone that Harriet O'Brien and Horace Hastings were having an affair. Were you aware of that?"

"I don't know where you got that information but to answer your question, I must say yes, I was aware of that.

Jeanne told me about that in confidence over a year or two ago.

"Do you agree with Jeanne that Horace was having an affair with Harriet?"

"If you mean having sex with her my answer would be yes. It was not an affair as far as Jeanne was concerned. She told me that Horace had met Harriet at the Laurel/Seaford football game last year and that he offered to take her home. Helen, Horace's wife was sick at the time, and she agreed."

"He then suggested that they stop and have a sandwich and coffee at the Spot Diner. Then after having the sandwich he drove her out on the Island and they had sex. From that time on, she and Horace were secretly having sex and Harriet was very concerned that Helen, Horace's wife, would find out."

"I told her to just quit doing it and she said that she was hoping that Horace would soon leave Helen."

"Why did you not disclose that on your previous interview?"

"I was under the impression that both of them had been raped and I knew in the case of Horace, he would not have had to rape either girl. They both would have been willing and happy to marry him. Then when Horace was killed I figured it would serve no purpose to make it known and that it would only hurt Horace's wife terribly."

"Do you think that Horace would end his marriage

with his wife, Helen, and marry one of those two women?"

"Oh yes, He and Harriet were planning on marrying, at least Harriet told me they were as soon as

Horace got a divorce from Helen. I think that they had already filed for divorce. She told me that they had to be careful that Helen didn't find out about Harriet because that would cost Horace a lot of money in the divorce agreement."

"What about Jeanne, how would she fit in? That is the real question. I told Jeanne she was just wasting her time. Jeanne simply said "well we will soon find out if it's Harriet or me."

"What did she mean by that?"

"She never told me, but I bet she would have told Horace. She was one of Harriet's best friends until she started dating Horace. Jeanne was dating Horace on the sly before Harriet got involved and Jeanne was really upset with Harriet. In fact I came close to telling you this before, but then Harriet was found dead and I was scared to death that Jeanne had someone do it."

When Carle got back to the station he disseminated the transcript of his interview with Thelma Webster and attached a note – "This is interesting I think we have finally found an answer to these murders. Try to obtain any additional input into these allegations and perhaps we can close these cases real soon. I am rather certain that we are about to come upon the answer to all of our questions."

"However the truth is that the case is weak, so we need to firm it up. I know that the DNA will give us the proof that we need."

The Coroner's report was received and confirmed that Harriet's body had no signs of abuse when the autopsy was performed at the time of her death."

"Harriet's clothing showed no signs of forced removal, there was no rips, tears, or stains, and the tight fitting slacks and undergarments were found still on the woman when found. The Forensic team suggested that it would have been very difficult to have been put on after the woman was raped and murdered. That would indicate that Harriet was not been raped."

"Jeanne's clothing showed extensive signs of forced removal, there were rips, tears, and stains, and her undergarments were found off the body near the marsh. There was no question on Jeanne, she had definitely been raped or prepared after death to appear as she had been raped."

Agent Bob Spedden was interviewing Fred Williams of the class and after reading the statement to him from the previous interview, he asked him if he had anything to add in view of the fact that Horace had been killed after he was last interviewed.

"I don't think that I can add anything except I did remember after we quit talking back then, that I did see Harriet talking to Oliver Hill who was standing by Harriet's red convertible. She was sitting in a car in front of the Deli on Market Street and that was the last time that I had seen her."

"I think I told you that I last saw her in a grocery store, but that was several days or maybe a week before the time I saw her talking to Oliver."

"I was surprised because Oliver really had little to do with all of us classmates. He is a strange individual."

"Can you recall when exactly that was? Was Harriet alone in her car or was someone with her?"

"No, I'm not sure of the exact date, but I do know that it was before the reunion, because I was thinking at the time that she was probably trying to get him to come to the reunion."

"Harriet was on the committee making the plans, and I think that Jeanne Records was with her. At least I think it was Jeanne. They were always together. I don't know if anyone has told you or not while they both dated boys, there was talk that they were lesbians."

"You mean Harriet and Jeanne?"

"Yes."

"That's something new; I have been led to believe that they were both very friendly with the boys, and dated them quite often."

"Well that's true I guess, but they dated them all but they didn't seem to be interested in any one boy. I suppose that is how that rumor got started."

"Come to think about it there's been talk around town that Harriet was having an affair with Horace Hastings."

"I have been told that too, but we have also been told that Horace was having an affair with another girl as well. Have you any information on that?"

"No, but I do know that Jeanne was upset over Harriet's death at the reunion. Horace was not with his wife and Horace was seen dancing with Jeanne most of the evening. I remember Henry Allison telling me at the reunion, "Jeanne didn't take long to fill Harriet's shoes did she?"

"What did he mean by that?"

"He was hinting that Jeanne was after Horace and his money instead of Harriet. Harriet had a reputation of being a gold digger, and Jeanne ran her a close second."

"Does Horace have a lot of money?"

"I really don't know for sure. I do know he has quite an operation at his farm. I have been told that he was selling twenty thousand chickens on the market each and every week of the year out of those big two story broiler houses he had built on his farm."

"A lot of the talk at the reunion was that Harriet was really after Horace's money and now Jeanne was after it. She was hugging all over him. Truth of the matter neither of them will ever get it because they were both raped and murdered. Poor Helen, Horace's wife, was at the reunion but she did not sit or dance with Horace all evening."

"Everyone said that they were separated and getting a divorce. She was at the reunion and had Larry Adams with her. Everyone thought that he was her lawyer probably because he was taking pictures."

"Her lawyer, are you sure he was a lawyer?"

"I'm sure that he wasn't now; because he was arrested and the newspaper said he owned an auto repair shop; but at that time somebody said he was a lawyer."

"They thought he was with her to get some information to help her case in the divorce. No one knew anything about him. All they said at the time was that he was from Salisbury, Maryland."

"Were they dancing together?"

"Not that I can remember, they were sitting at a table with several other couples, every time I looked at them."

"I took my wife over to meet Helen and I introduced my wife Gladys, to Helen. Gladys was from Tennessee and had never met her. Helen introduced the man with her simply as Larry Adams. She did not tell us his profession or where he was from. Just merely that his name was Larry Adams."

"He was the man that was arrested by your people of killing Horace. According to the newspaper he was not a lawyer after all. Could he have killed Horace for Helen? I was thinking that he may have done that for money."

"Yes, we know Larry he certainly was not a lawyer. Have you given any thought as to who may have killed the two ladies since we last talked?"

"Well after we last talked I tried to figure that out but after Horace was killed I just could not imagine any reason why or who could have done it except someone who did it for Horace's wife. She sure had a motive to kill all three of them. Maybe that guy from Salisbury who killed Horace killed the girls as well."

"Why do you say after Horace's death? Did you have someone else in mind before Horace was killed?"

"Well yes, I did. I was thinking that Horace may have killed the girls, so his wife would not find out that he had been running out on her, or that he may have hired someone to kill them; but when Horace himself was killed, that put an end to my thinking that way."

At the team's next daily meeting. Police chief Daley remarked that he was surprised how open the classmates were now as compared with the earlier interviews.

Agent Carle told them that it had been almost four months since the murders and they were no longer in fear of their own lives or involvement.'

"They are anxious to have it all closed, and are freely telling us things that they feared to mention before."

The team was told a report on the DNA test on Horace had been requested after Horace's death and a match had been made with that found on both Harriet and Jeanne and the fetus.

The team had suggested that the state Attorney General withhold publication of that report; but he refused to do so any longer because it was evident to him that Horace raped and killed the women.

He was anxious to announce publicly that the killer of the two women was Horace Hastings and that Horace was killed himself by Larry Adams of Salisbury, Maryland who was after Horace's money through his relationship with Helen. That would close the case.

Agents Carle and Spedden were opposed to making the announcements because everyone knew that Horace was dating both women and his DNA match did not prove that he had killed them. They felt that a jury would refuse to close the case without more proof.

"We have no evidence that proves he committed their murders."

The state's Attorney General reconsidered making his announcement and told them he would give them two more weeks to finalize their investigation before the news would be released. In the meantime he would not release those in jail.

Agent Carle told the Attorney General that they both felt that they needed to clear up a few items.

"Horace is our top suspect to this point but because the classmates are now talking so freely, and because we still have several other suspects that need to be cleared they needed just a little more time."

When asked who the other suspects were, he told those in attendance that they are in custody and their names should be kept confidential because if the names got out and published that just might kill their case.

It was agreed to withhold naming the suspects. Agent Carle stated that they had just received information that Oliver Hill, who was an earlier suspect, was reported just this morning as being seen with Harriet the day that she was reported as being murdered and was now thought to be the last person to see Harriet alive.

"Another two suspects are now in the picture again because we have proven that they returned to Seaford before heading to Florida; and, that conflicts with their statements when interviewed earlier. They were in Seaford when the two women were killed. They are Johnnie James and Henry Walker, both of Florida and are now in jail in Georgetown. They are both drug addicts who came to Seaford, with Harry Black all are suspects, and of course we have Albert Warrington still in our sights and need to confirm all of his testimony.

"Guys we have two weeks to get the murders solved. Let's get busy. Bob I want you to talk to those two Florida drug addicts. Jack, I would like for you to work on Horace as being the killer."

"I'm going to check on Oliver's testimony and use that text from other interviews to see just what he was talking about with Harriet for such a long time, that we have just learned about."

"The rest of you should take all the transcripts received to date and any interview that contains anything, anything at all, on these four suspects, I would appreciate a separate file be created so we can examine them for any inconsistency."

Helen arranged a second meeting with Horace's parents, his two brothers, Steve Cockran who worked on the farm for Horace, and her attorney Henry Faulkner.

Mr. Faulkner told the Hastings family that Harriet

had asked him to draw up the necessary papers to have the poultry business transferred to Horace's two brothers free and clear with no stipulations.

Both brothers were speechless for a few minutes, and as soon as they recognized that they had been given Horace's poultry business as a gift they rose and embraced Helen, and told her how pleased their families were that she did not hold anything against them for all she had been through over the past several years.

The lawyer then announced that Helen had deeded free and clear to Steve Cockran and his wife, the tenant home and nearby farm buildings plus 20 acres of land. This was the land where he and his family now lived and located at the southeast end of her property. Steve was Horace's farm manager and his right hand for five years. The lawyer stated that Helen had wanted him to have the property for his years of service to both Horace and Horace's parents

Steve's wife was also at the meeting and when she heard that announcement, she began crying and ran over to Helen, hugged her and thanked her.

"Miss Helen you are truly an angel, we have never owned anything in our lives. Thank you, thank you."

Mr. Faulkner continued and told them that Steve had told Mrs. Hastings he would continue to manage the farm for the brothers just as he had in the past for Horace and that he was to report to the brothers for questions or direction on problems that may surface and seek their guidance when needed.

The lawyer then told all present; that the transfers were given to the family and to Steve without stipulations.

Mrs. Hastings said that it was her hope to stay at the big farm house so that her children could grow up with their aunts and uncles and grandparents, but because she had found a position teaching children with learning deficiencies, for which she had been trained, in New Castle County and that position would require that she relocate to New Castle County.

"Having to leave the farm is the hardest thing that I have ever had to do. I have discussed this with Mr. and Mrs. Hastings and they have told me that they will agree to move into the big house. And that two of the four bedrooms will be available for me and my children's use on our frequent visits down state. So I have transferred to them lifetime ownership of the big house."

"Mr. Faulkner will serve as property manager for my six rental properties in Laurel and Seaford and all income from those properties is to be placed in trust accounts for the education of my children."

The next day Helen was in her yard when Steve Cockran, her farm manager, stopped his pickup and walked over to where Helen was sitting shelling some fresh pole beans.

"Miss Helen, I certainly do want to thank you for what you did for me and my family. I will certainly do my best in managing the farm. I never dreamed that I would ever become a property owner. Now that Horace is gone, you can always come to me for any problems you have."

"Well thank you Steve, You have always gone out of your way to help Horace and I and I have faith in you that you will continue to do so for the brothers. They are certainly going to need a lot of help now that they have the broiler business to run."

"Miss Helen, at the picnic the other day, I overheard your FBI man talking about that woman's red car that was found in Laurel, and I have been troubled lately with something that happened just before those women were killed."

"What's that troubling you?"

"Well, I don't know if it has anything to do with that red car or not, but Mr. Horace called me at my house late one night and told me that his pickup truck had stopped running and that he wanted me to come to Laurel to pick him up cause it wouldn't run and that all the repair shops were closed. He was going to have it repaired the next day."

"He asked me to pick him up in front of the Hotel Rigbie and he would wait there for me on the porch. Everything was closed up. I knew where that was so I went down and got him."

"The next day, I asked him if he wanted me to drive him down there when they got the truck fixed and he said that wouldn't be necessary and later that morning I saw his truck parked in back of the No.2, chicken house."

"I'm only telling you this because I heard that FBI man tell Mr. Miller that he wanted to hear about anything that may help him find out who had something to do with that red convertible that was found in Laurel."

"After Mr. Horace asked me to go to Laurel and pick him up, I happened to remember that I had seen a red convertible pick up Mr. Horace a few months ago at the No. 2 chicken house. I don't know if it was the same red convertible or not but I decided that I better tell you about that."

"Steve you should have told Mr. Carle about that."

"I wanted to do that, but I decided at the time, that I should not get involved with any of your guests conversations and decided I would tell you first."

"Steve, you are like family to me and my children, and I appreciate your feeling that way. I will tell Mr. Carle about what you have just told me. I am sure that he will contact you, and when he does, I want you to tell him anything that he asks. Don't be afraid to answer any of his questions. Ok?"

"Yes Miss Helen. I hope that it helps him to get the person that killed those women."

"So do, I Steve."

Helen immediately called Bill Carle on his cell phone, and Bill said he would stop by and talk with Steve within the hour.

"Steve, Mrs. Hastings told me that you might have some information that I was looking for and that she had given you permission to talk to me about that. Is that correct?"

"Yes, that's correct. I don't know if it will help you find

that killer or not; but I overheard you telling her guests at the picnic last weekend that you were hoping that anybody who had any information on a red convertible that was found abandoned in Laurel would get in touch with you and I do have some information about Mr. Horace and a red convertible."

"That's right Steve and Mrs. Hastings told me that she had told you that you should tell me anything that I asked of you."

"Yes, she did Mr. Carle."

"Great Steve, please tell me what you know about that red convertible."

"Well Mr. Carle, I don't know if it was the same red convertible or not, but what I told Miss Helen, was that I had seen a woman pick Mr. Horace up at the No. 2 chicken house some time ago. What I didn't tell Miss Helen was that I have seen her do that many times, because I didn't want Miss Helen to know about that. I told her that I had seen her pick him up one time. I didn't want to hurt her."

"I have been asked many times, over the past year or so, by people who knew I worked for Mr. Horace about Miss Helen and Mr. Horace's marriage problems. I told them I did my job and didn't know anything about their personal or business affairs."

"I understand that Steve, now tell me about what you told Mrs. Hastings about taking Horace to Laurel."

"Just after those murders and I really don't remember the exact date. I know it was just after that first woman was found murdered, because the newspaper said something about a red convertible and I wondered if Mr. Horace had anything to do with those murders because I had seen Mr. Horace with a woman in her red convertible many times."

"What really got me thinking, was that late one night, Mr. Horace called me on my telephone, and told me that his pickup had stopped running in Laurel, and he wanted me to come pick him up cause he couldn't get it fixed until the next day."

"It was about 2:00 o'clock in the morning and I wasn't happy about having to get dressed and drive all the way to Laurel, to pick him up, but I did it anyway."

"I was mad that he just didn't take a taxi. He had plenty of money. But I did as he wanted, I love my job here on the farm, and I knew better than to tell him to call a taxi."

"Now Mr. Carle, I want to tell you something that I did not tell Miss Helen. On my way back home from Laurel, I dropped him off at the motel where he was staying a lot of nights and where his car was parked. I then drove back to my house. I had to drive past the No. 2 chicken house to get to my house and I saw his old pickup parked behind the building and the security light was shining on it."

"I knew better than to mention that to Mr. Horace because he would know that I caught him in a lie. I just thought at the moment that he was just messing with that woman and it must have been her car that quit running and that was none of my business."

"That's it Mr. Carle, except a few days later, I asked him if he got his truck fixed and he said that it was fixed the next day. He even told me that it was a problem with the fuel pump."

"Thank you Steve, your story may prove very helpful. One question, where is Mr. Hastings truck now."

"Right in back of the No. 2 building where he always keeps it and where it was that very night I picked him up in Laurel. He rarely used it except to go to town when he needed some supplies. He used his car almost always to go anyplace else. I do remember wondering why he was driving it in Laurel at that early morning hour."

"Thank you Steve. For the time being, I would appreciate your not telling anyone about what you have just told me. If Mrs. Hastings asks, there is no need to upset her, just tell her that you told me what you already told her. We don't want her to worry or get upset do we?"

"No we don't, you just don't know all that she has done for me and my family."

After calling Helen and telling her that he and agent Spedden would be out to her farm in a few minutes. They returned to the farm with a local wrecker and a flat bed trailer and loaded up Horace's pickup and transported it to a local fenced car lot where it was being examined, for fingerprints and any other clues.

A small roll of wire cable was found under the seat

that was used on the farm on the feed conveyors of his chicken houses and a piece about three feet long was found in the glove compartment.

An examination by the forensic team found traces of blood on the bed of the pickup's cargo space, as well as on a pair of canvas work gloves. The wire was an exact match to the wire found on Jeanne's body.

It was determined that the blood on the gloves and on the wire were matches with that of both Jeanne and Harriet.

As soon as agent Carle got the information, he called Helen, "Helen, it's all over, all the murders have been solved now."

"Oh, that's wonderful Bill. Was it Horace who killed the girls?

"Yes, Helen, Horace did them. We have put all the pieces together now. We are certain that Horace killed Harriet, because Jeanne told him that Harriet was pregnant, Jeanne had told him that Harriet was after his money and adultery charges by your attorney would cause the judge to rule in your favor."

"He then killed Jeanne simply because he thought that she would know that he had killed Harriet. He simply wanted to shut her up and he made it look like rape in hopes that the murders would appear as a rapist. Harriet was always after Horace so Horace had sex with her and then made it look like rape after he killed her."

"We have determined that both women were after him. When Harriet told Jeanne that she was pregnant and that she was going to get Horace to marry her, Jeanne told Horace that Harriet had told her about the pregnancy and she was going to use that to get him to marry her."

"We feel that she told Horace that would hurt his divorce case, or Horace himself thought of that, we don't know for sure, but at any rate Horace was worrying about losing a large chuck of his wealth."

"Ironically it was his wealth that actually caused his death, because Larry Adams killed him in hopes of getting his wealth through you."

The suspects being held in jail were all released and the chief of police Daley called for a press conference who gave the newspapers the story that the Reunion Murders had been solved.

Bill Carle called Helen after the story had been released to the newspapers and asked her to have dinner with him that evening because he had been ordered back to the Wilmington office the next day.

He told her he was to appear before a news conference there on Wednesday of next week in Wilmington for the purpose of accepting his promotion to the Bureau's Chief position at the Branch office in Wilmington.

Helen told him how proud she was that he was to be promoted and, "Does that mean that you will be leaving us soon and have that bureau chief's job you were looking for?"

"Yes it does, my work has been completed here; but now I am hoping that you and the children will come to Wilmington with me. I can now spend most of my time in an office. Are you ready to make a commitment? I am. I hope you will join me. We can even live in New Castle near your new job if you wish."

"Is that some kind of proposal Bill?"

"Yes, it is Helen, I love you. Will you marry me?"

"As I have heard you say many times Bill, I can only tell you what is common knowledge, Yes, I love you too and I will marry you. I would like for Bob Miller and Kathy to stand up with us."

"That's a great idea Helen, and all of our children can repeat their roles for us."